THE SISTER PARADOX

JACK CAMPBELL

eBooks

Stratford, NJ

PUBLISHED BY
eSpec Books LLC
Danielle McPhail, Publisher
PO Box 493,
Stratford, New Jersey 08084
www.especbooks.com

Interior Graphic: Silhouette of unicorn © Soul wind, www.fotolia.com

Art Direction and Production: Mike McPhail, McP Digital Graphics

Copyeditors: Greg Schauer
             Wrenn Simms

Interior Design: Sidhe na Daire Multimedia
                 www.sidhenadaire.com

Dedication

To sisters,
without whom the world would
be much less interesting,
and at least a little less weird.

For S, as always.

CONTENTS

ACKNOWLEDGMENTS

MANY THANKS TO CATHERINE ASARO, ROBERT CHASE, Carolyn Ives Gilman, J.G. (Huck) Huckenpohler, Simcha Kuritzky, Michael LaViolette, Aly Parsons, Bud Sparhawk, and Constance A. Warner for their suggestions, comments, and recommendations. Also thanks to Sarah Damario for her help in coming up with a good title for the story.

Chapter One

Sister, What Sister?

With death on four legs and two wings heading straight for me, I finally turned to run, but slipped on the loose rocks and bare dirt on the edge of the large hollow. I caught a brief sideways glimpse of the charred, dead trees standing bare-limbed around the hollow as I landed on my shoulder, then I started cart-wheeling down the slope accompanied by a shower of rocks, pebbles, and dust. The slope seemed a lot longer than it had looked, but that was probably because I was picking up fresh bruises with every bounce on the way down. Finally, I slid to a stop at the bottom, accompanied by a pile of rubble and a cloud of dust that kept choking me while I tried to make the world stop going around in dizzy circles.

I'd just about managed to stop coughing and start seeing straight again when the dragon I'd been trying to run away from in the first place came slamming down to earth a few feet from me. Yeah, that's right, a dragon. The earth quivered with the impact, making the little collection of rocks and pebbles I'd brought down the slope with me jump around like they were panicking. The bones of those unfortunate enough to have gotten here well before me, carpeting the bottom of the hollow, also quivered as if given a few more seconds of life to be afraid. Up close, the dragon looked even bigger than I'd first thought, especially when it hissed and spread its jaws really wide. I hadn't managed to get up, but I tried to backpedal away. The dragon took two steps and stood right over me, jaws gapping.

If you're like me you've probably played one of those video games that claims to be totally realistic. Don't believe it. Having a real dragon standing over you with its jagged teeth dripping saliva is very, *very* different from whatever thrills you get out of a game. If there'd been an escape key, I'd have been punching it like crazy.

The dragon reared back a little and prepared to chow down on me. I stared at it, unable to move or think of any way out of this mess.

Did I mention that I wouldn't be in this mess if it wasn't for my sister?

Did I mention that I don't *have* a sister?

I guess I should start at the beginning. Like, this morning.

There's two things you have to know about me right from the start. First, my name is Liam. Liam Eagan. Second, I'm 16 years old. Third...okay, three things. Third, I don't have a sister. Or a brother. I'm the only kid in the family, the only kid my mother and father have ever had. It's been that way all my life, and it hasn't been all that bad. I mean, sometimes I'd wish I had a brother to toss a ball back and forth with or something like that, but I had friends I could hang around with instead. I never wished I had a sister. No way. Never.

There are advantages to being an only kid. No competition, for one thing. No fighting for the bathroom, or having someone else pawing my stuff, or complaining that they wanted something else to eat tonight when I wanted pizza. No one else asking Mom and Dad for expensive, but important junk. Just me.

This morning started off as usual. I lay in bed awhile after the alarm went off, took my time getting ready because I knew I wouldn't have anyone else hogging the bathroom, and slid down the stairs and into the kitchen with just enough time to spare.

Mom was already there, going over some stuff related to her job selling real estate. She gave me a quick glance. "About time you got down here. You're going to be late for school."

"No way," I assured her while I pulled out a box of cereal.

"Yes, way. Hurry your breakfast, mister," Mom ordered me.

I shrugged and dug in the cereal box until I had a handful, then shoveled it into my mouth before answering. "Okay, okay," I mumbled around my mouthful.

She gave me that look that moms get sometimes. "Nice. What happens when someone else in this house wants to eat that cereal?"

"You told me to hurry up, and nobody else in this house eats that cereal," I pointed out, quite reasonably I thought. "You eat that twigs-and-bark stuff and Dad just has coffee."

"That's not the point," Mom informed me. "Besides, what if we had a guest?"

That reminded me. "Hey, speaking of that, when can I have the spare bedroom?"

Mom looked baffled, though I couldn't imagine why. "The spare bedroom? You want to move into the spare bedroom?"

"I want the spare bedroom, yeah."

"What's wrong with your bedroom?"

"Nothing."

She waited as if thinking I needed to say something else, then sort of frowned at me. "Why do you want to move out of your bedroom and into the spare bedroom?" Mom said the words really slowly as if she thought I'd have trouble understanding them.

"I don't. I don't want the spare bedroom as a *bedroom*." Mom just kept waiting, so I explained even though it should've been obvious. "I need a place to hang out. You know, a room where I can play video games and music and stuff with my friends."

"You mean like your bedroom."

"No! Give me a break, Mom. I need another room for that stuff."

She just leaned back and stared at me. Finally, after several seconds, Mom shook her head. "Just what makes you think you can have two bedrooms for yourself?"

"Because there's no one else using it." Which was perfectly true. I didn't see how Mom could argue with that. "And it's not like you and Dad are doing anything with it."

Mom buried her face in her hands for a moment, I guess while she thought about what I'd said. "And where would guests stay when they come here?"

"There's that new hotel a few miles away."

She raised her face and stared at me again. "You want our guests to shell out money for a hotel and drive several miles back and forth to see us each day while you use the spare bedroom to do things you can do perfectly well in your own bedroom?"

The way Mom said it made it sound like I was being unreasonable. "If it's all that big a deal—"

"It's that big a deal." Mom leaned forward. "Hello, Earth to Mr. Liam Eagan. Have I got your attention? Listen carefully. You are not the only person in the world."

I knew that. "I know that!"

"You won't be getting the spare bedroom to use as a playroom. Forget it."

"All right, all right!" Obviously, I'd have to work on this a bit before Mom and Dad gave in. "But when we get the new TV—"

"Mister, you've got plenty of toys as it is."

Calling my stuff toys was not cool, but it did remind me of something. "Oh, yeah, I also need a new phone."

"A new phone?" Mom shook her head. "The one you've got is less than a year old."

"It's eight months old! There's a new model out with better memory! If I want to use the newest apps I need—"

"You don't *need* anything, Liam," Mom interrupted. "You *want* more stuff."

Oh, here it comes. The lecture about kids starving in Sudan, like that has anything to do with me.

But the clock in the living room bonged, causing Mom to check the time and dash for the door. "Don't be late for school!"

"No problem." And it wasn't. I've got the walk timed down to the second. I slid through the school door just before the bell rang.

James Rowland, my best friend, socked my shoulder. "Dude."

"Dude. Looking forward to playing Demon Disaster in death match mode after school?"

James shook his head. "Nah. Sorry."

"No?" I made a grabbing gesture toward him with both hands. "No? We've been planning this since Monday, remember?"

"I know, I know." James waved my hands away. "I'm stuck at home watching my little bro."

"Can't you ditch him?"

"He's three years old. He needs me. My parents are counting on me to watch him."

"So? We made plans!"

James shook his head again. "Sorry. If you had a brother or sister you might understand. Listen, you can come over to my place—"

"You don't have the latest game console! And your little brother would be nagging at us! How am I supposed to have fun while you—?"

"Look, we have to get together somehow to go over those book reports."

I hauled my mind away from sulking about no dual-Demon Disaster play tonight. "Book reports?"

"Yeah." James squinted at me like he wasn't sure I was serious. "Liam, the book reports are due tomorrow. We agreed we'd do the same book, that I'd read the first half of the book and you'd read the second half, and then we'd get together to write our reports."

"Oh, yeah. That was the report on..."

"Genghis Juan Feinstein and the Steam-Powered Airship of Senteri!"

"Dude, that book is huge! I thought it'd be a graphic novel! When did I agree to this deal?"

"About three weeks ago!"

Like I'm supposed to remember something I said three weeks ago? "I'll look something up on the web. Some, uh, notes or something—"

James interrupted me, looking seriously upset. "You know Mr. Weedle checks our stuff online to see if it's been copied! You know he insists on details from the books that aren't in online sources so he can be sure we read the books! How could you be so lame? You promised me, man!"

"I don't remember saying—Look, I'll get it read, and I'll call you tonight early enough so we can both get the reports done. Happy?"

"You're almost done reading your half?" James asked.

"Uh, yeah." What's two hundred pages of small type? I could skim through that in, say, half an hour. "I'll call you by...eight o'clock and—"

"Eight o'clock? Try seven."

"That won't leave me much play time before I start my homework," I complained.

James's face got a little red as he answered me. "Dude, sometimes the world does *not* revolve around you."

I should have known the rest of the day was going to be strange when my best friend started sounding like my mom. "What's that supposed to mean?" I asked as we walked to English class. It's not like James had put himself out when something important like playing a new game with me was involved.

Just then Tina Noe went by and I perked up real fast. "Hey!"

She glanced at me, then away. "Hey, yourself."

"Uh…" But Tina was already heading down the hall while I stood there trying to think of something cool to say.

"Wow," James whispered to me sarcastically, "she is *so* into you."

"She just has to get to know me better."

"She does know you."

"What does that mean?"

"You don't spend a lot of time worrying about other people, you know," James replied, apparently still steamed at me over the game thing and the book report thing.

"I do, too!" I tried to think of some examples, but we reached the classroom before I came up with any.

I wanted to forget all about the book report, but Mr. Wheedle started English class by reminding everyone about it. Like I needed another reminder. Then he said if anyone needed extra time we should let him know now.

I could feel James looking at me, but I sort of shook my head and stared at my desk. We could get it done. Probably. I mean, the report wasn't due until tomorrow, so dealing with any problems could wait until tomorrow, couldn't it? And maybe something would happen like Mr. Weedle being sick or me being sick, or whatever. Never stick your neck out if you don't have to. That's what I always say.

In English we started learning about something called splitting infinitives, which sounded like it might be fun to do, especially since Mr. Weedle said some grammarians insisted we weren't supposed to do it. But it just turned out to be something about organizing sentences, which is boring if you ask me, and Weedle said it was okay with him if we did it, so what was the point?

Boring, by the way, is Mr. Weedle's specialty. You've probably heard of teachers who can make any subject exciting and interesting. Mr. Weedle is sort of the anti-matter version of that. He could make anything boring. It wasn't really his fault, I guess. The tests force all the English teachers to go over the same old books chosen by a bunch of people who think reading doesn't count unless you have to force kids to do it.

So instead of worrying about obscure grammar rules and about society in a small town in 18th century England, I was thinking about what size TV to put in the spare bedroom when my parents gave in. But then one of the school office assistants stuck her head into the classroom. "Liam Eagan?"

Everybody looked at me, while I tried to think of anything I might've done lately. Or something I maybe didn't do and should've done. Aside from the book report thing, that is. Then Mr. Weedle pointed at me.

The office assistant made a "come here" gesture. "You're needed in the office." I started to get up. "Bring all of your books."

This looked bad, but I had no trouble looking confused instead of guilty, because was I sure hadn't done anything. James had gotten over his attitude enough to give me a worried 'what'd you do?' look, but all I could do was shrug to say I didn't know as I gathered my books up and dumped them into my backpack. The office assistant waited, tapping one finger on her arm impatiently until I got to the door, then led the way toward the office.

She led me right through the outside waiting area. I was so worked up by this time that I didn't even notice if anyone was in there. We went directly back to the principal's office, where the assistant knocked, looked in, then waved me in and closed the door behind me.

Ms. Emily Faith Meyer was the sort of woman kids did not mess with. She had this way of pinning you where you stood with her eyes, so that you felt she was reading your thoughts and knew everything you had ever dreamed of doing wrong. She sat there at her desk and frowned at me so hard that I wanted to yell "I didn't do it" even though I had no idea what "it" was.

Finally, she pointed to her phone. "We haven't been able to contact your mother or your father, Mr. Eagan."

That happens. "Mom usually keeps her cell on, but when she's doing real estate stuff she sometimes goes places where she can't get signal or has to shut off the phone. And Dad's on a business trip out of town."

"I see. Since we've been unable to contact your parents," Ms. Meyer paused as if trying to prolong my agony, "*you'll* have to take your sister home."

Have you ever heard something that's so completely strange that the words just don't make sense? This was like that. I heard everything Ms. Meyer said, every word as clear as a bell, and I couldn't understand it at all. Ms. Meyer looked at me, waiting for me to say something, so finally I just said, "Excuse me?"

"I said that you'll have to take your sister home."

"My...sister? Ms. Meyer, I don't have a sister."

"Mr. Eagan, I don't have time for games. You will take your younger sister home. This is for your mother." Ms. Meyer held out a sealed envelope. I knew what that was. I'd seen them, but never gotten one. Oh, man, Kari would really catch it when Mom saw that envelope.

Kari? Where had that come from? I didn't know anyone named Kari. "Ms. Meyer, I *really* don't—"

"Come along." I didn't have any choice but to follow Ms. Meyer into the waiting area.

And there *she* was, jumping up from a chair and smiling at me like she hadn't done anything. "Liam? You are Liam! Greetings to you, dearest brother!"

"Kari?" How did I know her name? How did I know *her*? I'd never seen her before. But as I stared at her, my mouth hanging open, I also knew that she was my sister. Which was crazy, because I didn't have a sister, but there she was standing in front of me, looking like somebody who had just left a Renaissance Faire or Live Action Role Playing game.

She had on a loose, long green shirt pulled in at the waist with a broad, leather belt that had a big metal buckle on it. The buckle was embossed with a unicorn's head, which should have looked very girly, but instead had this tough aspect that felt more *grrly*. Her pants were leather. Not shiny, stiff black leather, but light brown stuff that looked soft. Some sort of circlet running across her temples and all the way around held her hair in place. The circlet was made of braided threads that shone brilliantly white like metal even though they also looked soft. She was okay looking, I guess, though I didn't dwell on that with a girl I somehow thought was my sister. Ms. Meyer had called her my younger sister, but she couldn't be more than a year or two younger than me.

Kari stood there like she owned the world, one thumb hooked in her belt, grinning at me. "My dearest brother," she said again.

I wanted to yell "I am not" but all I could manage at the moment was "uh..."

The girl who couldn't be my sister, even though she sure felt like my sister, lost her smile as she turned toward Ms. Meyer and spoke like one adult to another. "I would like it returned now, if you please."

Ms. Meyer looked amazed. "Certainly not."

Kari's face tightened. "It is mine by right, given to me freely and entrusted to my care. You cannot take it."

"Young lady, it has been *confiscated* and it will *not* be returned." Ms. Meyer, obviously mad at the questions, glared at me before Kari could say anything else. "Take your sister home, now," she ordered, then stormed out of the office, probably looking for some kids to terrorize in the halls.

I could see Kari's eyes shifting around as if she were studying the area and the office assistants and vice principals standing around. Before I could think of anything else to say Kari beckoned to me and darted out the door of the waiting area.

"I hate it when you do that," I hissed at her when I caught up. I couldn't remember her ever doing it before, but I knew I didn't like it. "Who are you?"

She lost that angry, intent look for a moment as she smiled at me again. "Your sister."

"I don't have a sister!"

"Dearest brother. Of course you do, for am I not here? Now, follow me. We must act and then talk." More confused than ever, I followed her out the door of the school and around the corner of the building.

We stopped at the outside window to the principal's office. "What are you doing?"

"Getting back something which is mine." Kari peered inside. "There it is. We must hurry before she comes back, as I sense we should not create too large a disturbance. Give me a boost, dearest brother."

"I'm not your dearest brother!" But she was already pulling herself up and without even thinking I made a stirrup with my hands for her foot. Up close, I saw that her boot was leather, too. Very nice leather and really well made, with what looked like hand stitching and everything. "Mom and Dad give me such a hard time about how much *my* shoes cost, and then they get boots like this for *you*." No. Wait a minute. Who was this girl?

Kari glanced down at me before she went through the window. "These boots were crafted by the folk of Caderock, given to the White Lady as tribute and hence to me." She disappeared inside while I gaped up at where she had been, wondering why the sister I didn't have dressed and spoke like someone from a fantasy movie.

Somebody tapped me on the shoulder and I almost jumped out of my skin. When I came down, James was laughing at me. "What're you doing here?" I demanded.

"Physical education. I'm doing some independent walking until I get caught. So, what happened? Why'd you have to go to the office? Why are you so nervous?"

"She's in there." I pointed to the window.

"She? She who?"

"My...I don't know! She's some crazy girl who thinks she knows me!"

James gave me a funny look, and just then Kari swung herself out of the window. James looked up at her and grinned. "Oh. What'd Kari do this time?"

I grabbed his shoulders. "You know her?"

"Yeah. She's your sister!" James said, giving me a baffled look.

"I don't have a sister! You *know* I don't have a sister!"

"Um..." James frowned, looking more confused. "Yeah. But, isn't that Kari?"

"How do you know her name is Kari?"

"Because she's your sister," he protested.

Kari smiled as she dropped down from the window to what even I had to admit was a graceful landing. "I have it!" She raised her right hand to show off her prize.

A sword. A real long sword, not a toy. Three feet long, or maybe a little longer, the scabbard made out of leather that had been dyed deep blue, and decorated with lots of golden fittings and ornaments. The bright metal of the sword's guard shone in the sunlight, and the grip ended in a big, smooth stone more deeply blue than the scabbard.

James started laughing. "Oh, man! You brought a sword to school?"

Kari smiled wider as she fastened the sword scabbard to some leather straps and then slung it onto her back so the hilt stood up over one of her shoulders. Now Kari really looked like someone from a role-playing game. She reached up and back experimentally to grasp the sword, nodded to herself as if satisfied and tightened the straps. "Yes. Of course I had my sword with me. I could not believe that woman sought to take it. Is there no law in this land?"

"Old Lady Meyer is the law inside that building," James told her.

"A tyrant! But I have no time to deal with her now. It is well that I have recovered the Sword of Fate, for Liam and I shall have need of it."

"We will?" I asked.

"Of that I am certain, dearest brother. There is a task of some urgency which we must complete."

"A task?" Just what I needed. A sister I don't have shows up and starts telling me I have to do things. "With a sword?"

"Of course!" Kari insisted, then she frowned and looked at me in a puzzled sort of way. "Where is your sword? Did that woman take yours as well?"

I was still trying to come up with an answer to that when James pointed to Kari and laughed. "You nut case!" James turned to me, still laughing like crazy. "They go crazy if we bring in fingernail clippers to school, and your sister brings a sword!"

I didn't think it was all that funny. "She's not my sister!"

"Come on, Liam. It's Kari!"

"Are you saying you've met her before?"

James managed to stop laughing, instead looking confused. "Well, I...um...Hey, you better get out of here before Meyer finds out that Kari took that thing back."

"Yeah." That made sense at least, even if nothing else did. "James, you'd tell me if they were doing one of those reality TV things on me, wouldn't you?"

"Sure." He shrugged. "Nobody told me about anything like that."

"But this has to be—" But it couldn't be. Even if everyone else had decided to play along with some punk joke, how could it be a set-up if I also thought Kari was my sister even though I didn't have a sister? How could the TV people have messed up *my* mind?

I could only be sure of one thing: it was past time I took control of the situation. I'd risked getting into even more trouble by letting this girl lead me around here to break into Meyer's office. Now she was wearing a sword on school grounds and somehow I just knew I'd get blamed for it all if we got caught.

"See you, James. Come on, uh, Kari." This time I led. We had to go past the front of the school to get home, but I walked quickly, hoping no one would look out and see Kari and her sword.

Kari followed without a word of complaint and didn't object to walking fast, keeping up easily. "Do you fear encountering Lady Meyer again?" she asked.

"Yes," I replied. "Aren't you worried about that?"

"If she tries to take my blade again, I shall not be fooled and act with courtesy," Kari said. "Lady Meyer shall face the sharp edge of my steel instead."

This just kept getting better. I stopped for a moment and turned to face her. "No, she won't. Don't you dare point that sword at her or anyone else. What are you doing? Is this some kind of LARP thing?"

"LARP?"

"Live Action Role Playing. But they don't use real swords!"

Kari looked puzzled. "Why would anyone use a fake sword?"

"Because— Why do you always do this? Stirring up trouble, getting me involved, and then—" I tried to remember any times she had done that. Why was I so certain she had when I had never seen her before today?

"I did not start this quarrel with Lady Meyer," Kari said as she looked back at the school. "She is the ruler of that place?"

"Ruler?"

"Yes." Kari squinted. "I can read those letters! This is wonderful!"

"Yeah. Great. You can read."

"Hillcrest. It says Hillcrest," Kari announced. "She is Lady Meyer of Hillcrest. She is an evil overlord?"

I stopped walking again and looked at her. "Why don't you drop the act?"

"Act?"

"The whole dungeons-and-dragons thing!"

Kari frowned at me in puzzlement, then her expression lit with understanding. "She has a dungeon! Well, of course. But I see no trace of dragons near here."

The girl was hopeless. Or crazy. "Look, she is Ms. Meyer, principal of Hillcrest."

"Principle what of Hillcrest?" Kari asked.

"What?"

"You said this Lady Meyer was *principle of Hillcrest. Principle* means primary. But primary what?"

Definitely crazy. "No! No! You're doing this on purpose. Not princi-*ple*. Princi-*pal*. She's in charge."

"You had already told me that." Kari looked back at the school. "While inside I saw that she holds many in her thrall. They should be freed, but we have no time for that now."

I stared again. "Where did you come from, anyway?"

"I have always been here, Liam. In a way."

"No. No, you haven't. I might be a little confused right now, but I'm sure you haven't been here. I don't have a sister. I've never had a sister."

She smiled at me. "You have always had a sister, Liam."

"All right, then, if you're my sister, where've you been living? I *know* you haven't been living at my house."

Her expression became very serious. "I have been in Elsewhere."

"Elsewhere?"

"Yes. So the Archimaede says, though for all my life I thought Elsewhere was simply Here. But for me, it is Elsewhere, because

I was supposed to be in this Here," Kari explained, apparently thinking that she was making sense. "But something slipped, you see, and I ended up in Elsewhere instead. That's what the Archimaede told me, and Archimaedes know a great deal about such things."

"What's an Archimaede?" I asked.

"You have never met one?" she asked, surprised.

"No."

"How strange!" Kari twisted her mouth as she thought. The expression reminded me of someone else, but I wasn't sure who. "An Archimaede is much like a Dyrac."

"A Dyrac?"

"Yes. Though an Archimaede is much, much smarter than a Dyrac, of course."

"Well, that explains everything," I said. "Thanks."

Kari didn't notice my sarcasm. "You are most welcome. What is that growling sound? Are there many angry beasts near? Does the evil Lady Meyer keep them penned nearby?"

"Growling sound?" All I could hear was the traffic on the nearest road. "Look, let's just—" What? Take her home? The crazy girl from Elsewhere? But what else could I do? "Let's go on home."

"Home?" she said the word slowly. "Home. That would be delightful, if you would so honor me."

"Yeah. Delightful." I pointed off to the side and started walking again, not bothering to look at her. Maybe if I didn't look at her for a while I'd stop thinking she was my sister, or at least people who saw us wouldn't think we were together. "We'll take the shortcut through the park."

I didn't think it was all that much of a park, just a few acres of trees and some open areas with picnic tables and a playground and junk like that. I'd played there when I was younger, but for the last few years I'd only walked through the park on my way to other places. The big advantage of going through the park now, from my point of view, was the very small chance that anyone I knew would see me with Kari. If we had walked along the street plenty of people would have seen us together, which was the last thing I wanted. Right now I'd rather be seen in public with my parents than with Kari, and that was saying something.

"As you suggest," Kari agreed. "Have we far to travel? We must talk of our quest."

"Our quest?"

"Yes. I spoke of it earlier. It is very urgent."

"Uh...right." This had to be a TV show, or something on the internet. Sort of a LARP prank show. Though why Meyer would have cooperated with it, I couldn't imagine. "Home's not far, only a few minutes' walk."

"Minutes?"

"You don't know what minutes are?" Of course not. Fine. I'd play along for a while. "A very short time."

"Excellent! Lead on, dearest brother. Once there I shall explain the situation and we shall make our plans."

"Riiiight." Even if this girl hadn't been my sister (which she wasn't) I didn't think I'd want to make "plans" with a crazy girl who would bring a sword to school.

We strode along and soon enough were in among the trees. Kari had seemed a bit uncertain while we were surrounded by buildings, but now looked around with a big grin on her face. Some birds flew past, and a moment later I heard one trilling right next to me.

Nope. Not a bird. My crazy not-my-sister Kari, doing a really good bird impression.

I was about to make some comment when one of the birds suddenly flew down, perched on her raised arm, and started singing to her. I couldn't believe it.

Kari sang back to the bird. At least, that's what it sounded like. A conversation. Kari. Bird. Kari. Bird. They both sounded seriously happy, which started to really rub me the wrong way, because this was now crazy as well as weird.

"You know," I said darkly. "I have a pretty happy life right now and I don't need it messed up."

Kari paused in her talk with the bird to nod sympathetically to me. "I understand, dearest brother."

"No, I don't think you do, because otherwise you wouldn't be here and you wouldn't be pretending to talk to some bird while people can see us. You're already in trouble, you know."

The bird chirped something that didn't sound very nice at me, then flew off in a huff while Kari turned a once-more serious face toward me. "Oh, yes. I am quite aware of that! We are all in great trouble! After the Archimaede told me what I must do to preserve the walls between worlds I knew I must seek you out."

I blinked several times and focused on her again. "What?"

"The trouble. You were speaking of the trouble."

"I was talking about this!" I pulled the envelope from school out of my backpack.

She just looked curious. "What is it?"

"A letter to Mom from Principal Meyer telling her you took that sword to school and probably saying you're going to be suspended for who knows how long!"

"Really?" Kari walked a few more steps, looking ahead as she thought. "Suspended? Is this how Lady Meyer punishes her victims?"

"Usually, yeah."

"How does she suspend them? By rope or chain or on a platform? And just for having my sword with me! How else was I supposed to travel? Unarmed against the perils of the road? This Lady Meyer of Hillcrest really is an awful tyrant, it seems to me."

Great. The sister I don't have shows up from Elsewhere and doesn't have a clue. "Yes. That's right. You've got it. Now let's drop that subject."

"Very well, dearest brother. But you brought it up, after all."

"I didn't...never mind."

Kari gave me a questioning look, then shrugged. "Very well. How much longer do we expect to be journeying?"

"It's just a little ways farther. To *my* home."

But she didn't get my rather broad hint, of course. Instead, Kari suddenly smiled again. "Home." She said the word in kind of a funny way, like it was special just to say it. "We shall be there soon?"

"Yeah. I guess we'll just have to wait there until Mom gets back and then I'll hand you over to her." This definitely fell into Mom's area of responsibility. I had to wonder how Mom would react to my suddenly having a sister, but if I did have a sister then Mom must have had something to do with it, right?

Funny she had never even mentioned it though. You'd think a mother would bring up something like a sister.

"Mom? You mean Mother!" Kari seemed momentarily lost for words, then she started doing that bird-singing again and it sounded like every bird in the area chimed in. Some more of them flew down and perched on her arms and shoulders while they all sang together.

My friends will sometimes talk about how strange their sisters can be. I didn't have much personal experience with sisters, having only acquired this one about half an hour ago, but I didn't remember any of my friends ever saying their sisters did anything like the stuff Kari had been doing in the very brief time since I'd met her.

Fortunately, I didn't yet know that from that point on things were going to get a lot weirder.

Chapter Two

Mom, Meet Your Daughter

"HI, MOM. YOU'RE HOME."

She was in the kitchen, sitting at the breakfast table going through today's mail. Mom glanced at me with a questioning expression. "Yes. I just got back from showing a house. I think I made a sale. Why are *you* home from school so early, Liam?"

I sat down opposite her, trying to figure out how to explain the situation, and only coming up with the truth. "The principal made me bring my sister home."

Mom gave one of her heavy, exasperated sighs. I'm not sure why, but it seems I've been hearing more and more of those the last couple of years. "What really happened?"

"Seriously, Mom. I had to bring my sister home."

"Gee, and here I've thought you were an only child all these years."

"Mom, I'm not joking."

"Really." She was looking at me like she was trying to figure out what I was up to this time. "Liam, I'd know if I'd ever had a daughter. Believe me. And your father never had any other children, either. Nor have we ever adopted anyone. You *don't* have a sister."

"I *know* that, but everybody else thinks I have a sister, and the principal made me bring her home!"

Mom drummed her fingers on the top of the kitchen table, her mouth twisted in that way it does when she's thinking. "What are you trying to accomplish here?"

"I'm trying to tell you the truth!"

"Fine, young man, if you had to bring your sister home, where is she?"

"Right out there. That's her." I pointed out to the backyard, where I'd left Kari talking with a couple of sparrows she had met on our way inside. "I thought you wouldn't be home yet so when she stopped to talk to some birds, I said fine."

Mom had her that's-about-enough-of-this face on by now, but she stood up and looked out the window. Mom just stood there, staring, her expression getting more annoyed and sort of upset. Had Kari disappeared back into Elsewhere and left me stuck with an empty backyard and a totally ridiculous story? "Mom, I—"

"That's enough, Liam," Mom said in the kind of voice that made it clear she meant it. "What's the meaning of this?"

"I swear they told me this girl was my sister and—"

"That's not what I mean and you know it!" Mom turned a real glare on me. "Why is Kari wearing a sword? Is that why she got sent home from school?"

I stared at her for a moment, realized my mouth was hanging open, then managed to nod. "Uh...yeah."

"Why did you let her wear a sword to school, Liam?"

I stared at Mom again, feeling seriously persecuted. "You're yelling at *me*? Why don't you ask *her* why she wore a sword to school?"

"Because you're her big brother and—" Mom's voice cut off abruptly. Her eyes got really big and her mouth hung partway open as she stared back at me.

"Are you okay, Mom?" I asked.

Mom moved her mouth a couple of times without making a sound, her expression now half-scared and half-stunned, then slowly turned her head back to look out the window at Kari again. "Your...*sister*?" Mom's voice sounded really, really strange.

"Uh...yeah. That's what everybody keeps saying, anyway."

"You don't have a sister!"

"I know!"

"Then what—? Wait a minute." Mom closed her eyes, shook her head as if dizzy, then looked outside again. "Kari?" she whispered, then gathered herself and yelled out the window. "Young lady, you stop talking with those birds and get in here this instant!"

"Mother?" I could hear Kari's answer, filled with emotion. "Yes, honored Mother!"

A moment later I heard Kari banging at the outside door, rolled my eyes, and got up to open the door for her since she apparently didn't know how to turn the doorknob. Kari rushed past me into the kitchen, stood staring at Mom with an awestruck expression, then actually went to one knee and clasped her hands together in front of her. "Honored Mother," she said. "You are so beautiful."

Mom got a funny look on her face as she stared at Kari. "Don't...don't try to talk your way out of this. Where...where have you been?"

"In your garden, honored Mother," Kari breathed, her expression still enthralled as she gazed at Mom.

I sat down again. "It's the backyard," I corrected Kari.

"No!" Mom said to Kari, apparently ignoring me instead of giving me the usual 'don't use that surly teenager tone of voice' speech. I never thought that *not* hearing that speech would annoy me. "Not just now," Mom added. "How...how old are you, Kari?"

"I have seen the seasons pass fourteen times."

"Fourteen years?" Mom whispered. "You're fourteen years old?"

"Yes, honored Mother."

Mom swallowed and nodded, staring back at Kari. "Where have you been for the last...fourteen...years?"

I had been watching them with a growing feeling of being left out, which I'm totally not used to because I'm the *only* kid in this family. So now I answered in a voice that I admit had more than the usual surly teenager tones. "She's been nowhere."

"*Else*where," Kari corrected. "I have been Elsewhere."

"Elsewhere, nowhere. Same difference."

Kari shot me a baffled look. "Honored Mother, I believe that Liam is mocking me."

"Stop mocking your sister, Liam." The instant Mom got through saying that she shook her head again and stared at us. "Did I just say that?"

I nodded, fighting down a burst of irritation that Mom had immediately sided with Kari. "You said it."

"What am I going to tell your Father?" Mom wondered. "No, wait. Kari, have you ever met your father?"

"No, honored Mother."

"Lucky for him," Mom muttered. "If he'd— How could I have had a daughter and not known it?" she wailed.

"I came to be in the wrong place," Kari admitted, "through no fault of yours."

"But—" Mom studied Kari carefully. "I know it's true, but I don't know how I know that, or how it can be true."

I looked at both of them. "There is sort of a resemblance between you two," I had to admit.

Mom stared at Kari again, wordless for a moment, taking in her clothing. "Why are you wearing a sword, Kari?" Mom finally asked. "Yes. Let's focus on that. Tell me why you have a sword. Where did you get it?"

"It was given to me by the Lord and Lady of the Great Fen," Kari explained.

"The Great Fen?"

"Between the Mountains of Ogreholm and the River of the Naiads."

"Oh." Mom gave me an accusing look, as if I somehow had something to do with the Ogre Mountains and the Naiad River. "And why did you wear it to school?"

"I need it, honored Mother," Kari said. "The Sword of Fate carries an enchantment which gives it great power in time of need. I will need it on an urgent quest which Liam and I must undertake."

"Oh"," Mom repeated. "A quest. Is this one of those game things like your brother plays on his computer all the time?"

Kari frowned in puzzlement. "Com-pew-ter, honored Mother?"

"You don't know what a computer is?"

"Alas, no, honored Mother. You say my brother plays on it. Is a com-pew-ter then a musical instrument? I play the minstrel's harp well, though I have not mine with me. But I have not played the com-pew-ter."

Mom reached over and grabbed a chair, then sat down in it pretty hard and just kept staring at Kari. "That's nice. Musical training is very...I'm sorry, but this is...why do you keep calling me honored Mother?"

Kari bit her lip, her eyes shining again as she looked at Mom. "It is only proper to use polite terms of address to those we honor."

"Polite? You're saying it's good manners?" Kari nodded and Mom somehow looked even more stunned than before. "I have a teenage daughter *and* she has good manners?"

I wasn't sure why, but that sounded like a crack aimed at me, and *I* hadn't done anything. "Hey!"

Mom looked at me for a moment like she couldn't remember who I was, which really ticked me off. "Liam," she finally said, like she had only then recalled my name. "Why didn't you tell me about her?"

"I did! I sat here and said, I had to bring my sister home, and you kept saying, you don't have a sister, and I kept saying, I know, but she's here anyway, and you kept saying—"

"All right!" Mom interrupted. "Kari, how do I know your name and who you are even though I don't know who you are?"

Kari scrunched her face up and spoke with care, as if she were trying to say something just right. "It is complicated, honored Mother. You did not chose to give me up. It happened without your knowledge or consent, and because of that I am told that a small part of me has always been here and you have always known it."

Mom listened intently, started to nod, then shook her head. "I'm so confused. Stand up, Kari. Why are you kneeling?"

"It is only proper to render respect to those we honor."

"You're polite," I said sourly. "We get it."

Kari came to her feet, looking at Mom with a worried expression. "Are you feeling all right, honored Mother? You appear distraught."

"Distraught?" I asked, laughing at the word.

"Honored Mother, Liam is—"

"Will you kids stop it!" Mom snapped. "You two know I don't like it when you fight with each other."

"Mom," I said, getting more upset myself. "I'm pretty sure this is the only time I've ever fought with her around you!"

"That's right, isn't it?" Mom nodded slowly, her face pale now. "I need to lay down for a while."

Kari reached out and touched her hand gently. "Is there any way I can assist you, honored Mother? Are you not happy that I am here?"

Mom stared for a moment at Kari's fingers where they rested on her wrist, then smiled. "Yes, Kari, I am happy. But

I need a little time to absorb this. This is...it's...a little un-usual."

"The Archimaede said it might be difficult for you."

"W-what's an Archimaede?"

"They're a lot like a Dyrac," I told Mom.

"But much, much smarter," Kari added quickly.

"Oh." Mom, still pale, stood up and pointed toward her bedroom with a shaking finger. "I really need to lay down."

I finally remembered the envelope in my backpack. "I've got—"

"Not now, Liam. Go play with your sister." Mom's eyes looked funny again. "Your sister. Just go in there. Both of you. I'm going to rest for a while. I'm sure I'll feel better in a little while." She gave Kari a look like she wasn't sure Kari would still be there in a little while. "Don't...don't leave."

Kari smiled at her. "We may have to leave, but I will be back if you wish it, honored Mother."

"Yes. Yes, I do wish it." Mom tottered off to the bedroom, talking to herself under her breath, while I led Kari into the living room. I flopped down on the sofa while Kari wandered around, giving little exclamations as she focused on different objects. At one point she walked around the television, looking at it from different angles before peering into the front. "This is not a very good mirror," she said.

"Yeah. I'm trying to convince Mom and Dad to get a new one that's a lot better." I watched her for a while, trying to figure her out. Who gave her permission to horn into my life, anyway? And what was with the way Kari had acted toward Mom? Was she trying to make me look bad? "Kari, why were you looking at Mom like that?"

"At Mother? Like what?"

"Like she was the most wonderful thing you'd ever seen, or something."

Kari tilted her head as she stared at me. "She is the most wonderful thing I have ever seen."

"Uh, Kari, maybe Mom's kind of pretty, I guess, like you said, but she's not—"

She laughed. "Liam, you are mocking me again. I am learning about you, you see! Do you actually think I would believe that you do not know just how wonderful a thing a mother is to her child?

I have seen elven lords and ladies in their full glory under the stars, holding court with unicorns, hippogriffs, wyverns, and other charmed creatures while the moon struck sparks from the jewel-embedded walls of their castles, and it was *nothing* compared to the moment I first looked into my mother's eyes."

Kari paused, her face shining at the memory, while I gaped at her and tried to figure out if she was serious. Sure, Mom's all right. Most of the time, anyway. But I couldn't match the woman I had known for my whole life with this vision that Kari claimed she had seen. "But she's just Mom."

"'Just Mom'? Liam, you cannot play me for such a fool. No one could be so blinded by familiarity as you pretend to be."

For some reason I didn't want Kari to think I took Mom for granted. Because I don't. No way. At least, I'm pretty sure I don't. I mean, I'm always telling her...uh...hi in the morning, sometimes at least, and bye when I leave, sometimes, and...uh...what's to eat, Mom? I do say that a lot. And...uh...

All of a sudden, I felt sort of rotten. "Man."

"Excuse me?" Kari looked around.

"What?"

"You addressed another man, but I do not see another man here."

Another man? Which meant she thought I was...? Maybe Kari wasn't so bad after all. "No, I just...realized that I need to say thank you to Mom a little more often."

Kari had stopped to look at a family picture, me about six years ago along with Mom and Dad, all dressed up for the portrait. I think I look like a geek in the picture, but Mom thinks it's nice. "This is Father?" Kari asked.

"Yeah. He's out of town right now. Dad has to travel for business sometimes."

"What does he do for business?"

"He—" Right about then I realized that I didn't really know. "He works for...." Time to change the subject. "Let's just say for the sake of argument that you really are my sister..."

"You know that I am, dearest brother."

I shook my head in disbelief. "How come I know that? And if you've been somewhere, nowhere, wherever—"

"Elsewhere."

"For fourteen years, why did you show up here today?"

Kari's expression grew solemn and she sat down on a footrest, crossing her legs and shrugging her shoulders to settle the sword scabbard on her back with the ease of long practice. "It has to do with the walls between worlds. Do you know of them?"

"No."

"Oh." She furrowed her brow in concentration. "What did the Archimaede say? All worlds are here. At the same time. But the walls keep them apart, so even though they are all here, they stay separate in different places."

"You mean like the multi-verse? Lots of different dimensions coexisting but separate?"

"Perhaps it is." Kari gestured with her hands. "I told you I ended up in Elsewhere because something slipped. You do not remember? I did tell you. I know I did."

"Okay, okay. You told me."

"According to the Archimaede, who must know of this multi-verse of yours, other things from here have slipped into Elsewhere as well. Too many of them. Because of that there is what he called a strain, as if the fabric of the walls is being pulled apart."

I hunched forward, half-searching her face for signs she was kidding and half-searching for any hidden cameras that I still suspected might be filming this for the world's amusement. "What kind of things have slipped into Elsewhere?"

Kari threw up both hands. "Small objects, apparently. Though I am not nearly so small as I once was. Things that have gone missing here because they ended up in Elsewhere."

I couldn't resist. "You mean like socks and TV remotes?"

"Socks and what?"

"TV remotes." She just stared at me. Which made sense when I remembered that she had thought our TV was a bad mirror. Apparently, Kari had never heard of television. How weird is that? "Never mind. It was supposed to be a joke."

"Oh." She smiled in the way people do when they're trying to be polite. "I suppose people in your world lose these ree-motes sometimes? Then you understand what I am speaking of. Sometimes something which is lost is truly lost, losing its place in one world and finding a resting place in another. This sort of thing happens because even though it is very improbable, it is not impossible, and what is not impossible must occur at times in the infinity of possibilities. So says the Archimaede."

That made a strange kind of sense. "That sounds like quantum physics. You mean if there're' infinite possible worlds then anything that *could* happen sooner or later *will* happen."

"Just so! The Archimaede must know your kwan-tum fiz-icks. But, every time something slips into the wrong world, it causes a strain on the walls between those worlds. It belongs in one world, but it exists in another world, and so its wave crosses the walls and weakens them." Kari sighed, looking sad for some reason. "So those things must be returned to their own world."

"Wave? Like wave function? I know I've heard of that." I spread my own hands. "So what does this have to do with us?" Right after I said "us" I realized that I had actually spoken of Kari and I doing something together. This girl was slipping herself right into my nice little part of the world. I needed to do whatever she needed done so she would go back to nowhere and let me get on with my life and what I wanted to do.

Unaware of my thoughts, Kari smiled at me. "We have to get those objects from Elsewhere and return them to here. That will relieve the strain. It is a quest, Liam. The quest I spoke of. Our quest. And a very important one, as you must see."

"Hold on." I got up and started walking around, unable to sit still for this story. "We? *We've* got to get these objects? Who says?"

Kari hopped up from her footstool and stood in front of me. "It is very simple. I am one of those things which holds a tie to my home. I can cross from here to Elsewhere because I really belong here, but I have been living in Elsewhere so I belong there, too."

I nodded. "My sister lives in a world of her own, but she can visit this one."

"Exactly so! But how can I recognize the inanimate things from here that have slipped into Elsewhere when I know nothing of here? You must come with me so you can identify them."

That didn't sound too hard. "But why me?"

"Because you are my brother! I could not bring a stranger along. The walls would not let anyone else pass through with me."

"Wouldn't me being in Elsewhere hurt the walls even worse?"

"The Archimaede told me that when something new arrives it at first has little effect, only later growing more dangerous.

Since our quest must be completed quickly, you should not be in Elsewhere long enough to cause a problem."

Something else was bothering me. "Kari." I raised a forefinger for emphasis and spoke slowly. "I met you about an hour ago for the first time. Just how do you define stranger?"

"Liam." She shook her head. "Would you know a stranger when you first laid eyes upon them?"

"Well, maybe not. What happens if we don't do this?"

"The walls between our worlds will fail. I do not know exactly what will happen then. The Archimaede said it would be terrible."

I thought about that. "Our two worlds coexist in the same space, but the walls keep them separate. So if the walls fail, our two worlds will both be here in the same space. Two universes, occupying the exact same space."

"Do you know what will happen?" Kari asked.

"Yeah. I think so. A really, really, really big explosion." An explosion big enough to annihilate two universes. That would make a cool special effect, but the real thing wouldn't leave anyone around to enjoy the spectacle. "If your Archimaede is right, we do have to get this done."

It wouldn't be that bad, would it? Go to some place with elves and wyverns and stuff and pick up a few things. Cool. Why not? How dangerous could the place be if Kari had lived there all of her life? "Does everybody have swords in Elsewhere?"

"Almost everyone," Kari agreed. "No one would leave home without their sword at hand."

Aha. And her sword had all those golden decorations and that big, fake jewel in the hilt. Swords must be like friendship bracelets here and all the girls in her nowhere wore them. Girls and their fashion stuff.

Besides, Kari didn't really belong here, and she wasn't going to leave unless I agreed to this. I mean, Mom had been really upset. And Mom had sided with Kari even though *I* was the kid in this family, which just showed how much Kari being here confused things. I had to get rid of Kari for Mom's sake as well as my own.

I thought I heard James saying "sometimes the world does not revolve around you." Well, maybe the world didn't revolve around me, but this house did. What was so wrong about wanting things to stay that way?

All I had to do was go with Kari, get the stuff we needed, see some cool things, and then leave Kari back in her own little world to annoy everybody there instead of annoying me here. It sounded like a good plan. Well, at the time it sounded like a good plan. How was I to know that Kari had left out a few important details? "How do we get to this Elsewhere place?"

"It is not hard if you know the way," Kari said eagerly. "But we will have to walk. Unless Mother knows a unicorn! Does Mother know a unicorn?"

"Uh...no. We don't even know, I mean, have a horse."

"Oh. A horse would not work anyway because horses would panic in the place between worlds," Kari explained.

I should have keyed on that little revelation, like wondering what would make horses panic in that place between worlds, but I was too busy being satisfied with my clever plan to get rid of her.

"Surely you don't walk everywhere?" Kari asked.

"No. Mom's car takes us places."

"Car?" Kari looked puzzled. "Is that a creature of some kind?"

"No. Cars are made of metal and stuff."

"Metal? But it takes you places? Is a car a magical thing?"

I laughed. It was funny seeing Kari talking one minute about what sounded like high-end physics and the next minute being confused about the simplest things. "Magical? Not even. The ads say they're magical, but that's not true."

"Ads? These ads are not truthful?"

"Not really," I said. "They lie all the time."

"Thank you, dearest brother," Kari said solemnly. "I appreciate your warning me of the dangers of your world. I will remember if we should encounter any of these ads to be wary of them. Are they common? Are we likely to encounter any ads?"

I wasn't sure what she was talking about this time. Dangers? "Ads? Of course we'll run into ads. They're everywhere. This house is full of them."

"Everywhere!" Suddenly, Kari looked worried, glancing around. "This house is full of these ads?"

"Yeah. Every house is. I'm sure there's a bunch in this room."

"In this room?" Kari backed toward the nearest wall, looking rapidly from side to side. "Where? Are there any nearby?"

I looked around the room. "I don't...oh, yeah." There was a magazine face down on the coffee table, and the back cover had one of those *buy this and you'll be rich and happy* advertisements. I pointed. "There's an ad."

"Where?" Kari jumped backward, drawing her sword in a flash and looking wide-eyed in the direction I'd pointed. "Where is it?"

"On the table—"

"They are invisible! And dishonest!" She was holding the hilt of her sword with both hands, the point leveled in the general direction of the coffee table.

"No, no! Wait a minute." I stayed well away from the sword, hoping that Mom wouldn't pick that moment to walk into the living room. Maybe that sword was just a fashion accessory, but the edges and point looked pretty sharp from where I stood. "Ads aren't dangerous. Not unless you believe them."

Kari kept her sword out and gave me a skeptical look. "You are certain?"

"Yes. Really. You can put that away. Please put that away."

She slowly straightened and put the sword back into its scabbard with one smooth gesture that impressed me despite myself. "I am not sure how you manage to live in a world overrun with invisible creatures who are always trying to deceive people," Kari said.

"I guess you get used to it."

"I do not see how." Kari settled her sword and nodded to me. "Are you ready to go?"

"Go? Now?"

"Yes, now!" Kari insisted "Our time is limited! The walls between worlds are strained! We must go and begin finding the objects!"

CHAPTER THREE

THROUGH THE WALL OF WORLDS TO ELSEWHERE

"WE CAN'T JUST WALK OUT WITHOUT TELLING MOM!" Though I wasn't sure what I'd tell her. *I'm going for a walk to another world? It has something to do with saving the universe, I think, but it doesn't sound dangerous?*

You have to admit that it didn't sound dangerous *then*.

Mom's aggrieved voice floated into the living room. "You kids stop arguing!"

"Okay, Mom," I called back softly. Then I glared at Kari. "See what you did?"

"I did not! What are you talking about?"

I held up my hands in a shushing motion. "When Mom uses that voice it means she's got a really bad headache."

"Oh." Kari nodded sympathetically. "And you say you have no unicorn to assist. Should we then call on a healing mistress, or do you have potions already here?"

"Uh...we've got, uh, potions handy, yeah," I said. "Aspirin."

"As-prin? It is powerful?"

"Yeah. Extra-strength."

"That is well." Kari looked worried. "Are you certain it is not the work of an enemy? A curse perhaps? Does Mother have enemies?"

"Not that I know of." *None that could hurl curses, anyway.*

"That is good to hear. Still, I am concerned. What could have caused our honored mother to have a serious headache?"

"Maybe having a fourteen-year-old daughter show up out of nowhere had something to do with it?"

"*Elsewhere.* I have been in Elsewhere. Why can't you get it right?"

"I'll try. Just wait a sec. Mom? Uh, Kari and I are going for a little walk. Okay?" Hey, it was the truth.

"Okay, Liam," Mom replied. I gestured to Kari and we started to go, then Mom spoke again. "Liam?"

"Yeah, Mom?"

"Make sure you bring your sister back with you."

Rats. "Sure. No problem. Later." That complicated things. I still wanted to ditch Kari, but now if I did Mom would probably get all upset at me even though I couldn't very well bring back my sister when I didn't even have a sister to begin with. Mothers don't always pay attention to simple logic like that.

Then again, if Kari decided she didn't want to come back, it wasn't like I could make her come home with me. Now that I thought about it, Kari hadn't said anything about staying here. Why would she want to stay here if she really lived in a place with elves and unicorns? The thought cheered me up quite a bit. "Okay, I'm ready."

"Just a moment," Kari said as she rapidly braided her hair and pinned it up. How do girls do that? "I like my hair down usually, but I must be ready in the event we are threatened," she explained.

Only one word of that had registered on me. "Threatened?"

"Threatened," Kari confirmed as if that were the most natural thing in the world.

Again, a pretty clear clue that I should have paid attention to, but didn't. Afraid that Mom might hear words like "threatened" and stop us from leaving, which would stop me from ditching Kari back in Elsewhere, I gestured for quiet, then pointed Kari out the back door. She slipped through the kitchen so quietly that I couldn't even hear her moving. Nice trick. I stared for a moment, not wanting to admit that I'd been impressed again. By the time I caught up, Kari was standing in the backyard, glancing around, biting her lower lip. She pointed off to one side and started walking. I hustled to catch up as she warbled something to the sparrows, who chirped back at her.

"How do you do that?" I asked her. "Talk to birds?"

"It is because I have been Elsewhere. The Archimaede says many people have abilities like that, but in their own worlds they never develop them."

I wondered what special ability I might have had. Nothing to do with math, judging from my experience in this world. "What do you talk to birds about, anyway?"

Kari grinned. "All kinds of things. The birds can see in your bedroom window, you know." She giggled, while I felt my face getting warm. I mean, it's not like I have all these big secrets, but I still didn't want to have to worry about a bunch of birdbrains spying on me.

Kari talked on, walking far enough ahead of me that she hadn't noticed me flinch. "But the birds also like to talk about the world, about the patterns of life around them. And they want to hear about us. They see us all the time, doing things, and they want to know why we do them and what the things mean."

"Huh." As far as I was concerned, the birds should mind their own business. Whatever I was doing in my own room and why I was doing it was my business. I gave the sparrows a hostile look as we passed by them, then almost tripped over a tree root as I followed Kari. She went around another tree and then another. That made three trees and the last time I'd looked we only had two in the backyard. I looked back toward the house and could see nothing but more trees behind us. "Where'd the house go?"

Kari didn't look around. "We are going to Elsewhere. The house is not in Elsewhere."

That made sense. I guess. Elsewhere sure had a lot of trees, though. I began to wonder how I'd be able to find the objects we were looking for if they were all scattered around a forest like this. "Should I start looking for stuff?"

This time Kari paused and gave me a warning glance. "We are not even close to being there. But you ought to speak more quietly." Instead of that annoyingly cheerful voice I'd been hearing most of the time since meeting her, Kari sounded serious. Like *she* was in charge. Like she had the right to give *me* orders.

So she thought she'd get to run things, huh? I'd have to set her straight on that. "Why?"

Kari frowned because I hadn't bothered keeping my voice down. "Quietly, please, Liam. Basilisks haunt the walls between worlds. I really don't want to attract their attention and neither do you."

"Basilisks?" My voice got a lot quieter. I'd had an argument all ready to go, but that argument hadn't contained anything about what I'd thought were mythical monsters. "Actual basilisks? They're real?"

Kari looked at me like she couldn't believe I was seriously asking the question. "Of course they are real."

"The kind of basilisks that are giant snakes and turn anyone who looks at them into stone?"

"That is the only kind of basilisk there is." Kari raised one finger to her lips in a shushing motion and beckoned me onward.

Okay, if there were real basilisks running around, or rather slithering around, then maybe it wouldn't hurt to let Kari run things just a little. That was when I first started to suspect that this little quest of Kari's wouldn't be quite the cake walk I had expected. But I would never have guessed what was in store for us. Like that dragon, which we *will* get back to, I promise, even though I'm not personally in any hurry to get back there.

The forest had started out feeling sort of like a park, with regular-looking trees, grass on the ground, and everything pretty open. But as Kari continued walking it kept getting wilder and wilder until the trees loomed up on all sides, very tall and with trunks so thick it seemed as if nobody had ever cut down a tree here. The grass got wild and patchy, with bigger and bigger bare areas where nothing but fallen branches and leaves covered the ground. Every once in a while, a bird would flit down and chirp something to Kari, and then she would head off in a slightly different direction.

Birds didn't seem like a good substitute for GPS. I hauled out my phone and popped it open to check our position, only to find an "out of area" notice and no signal bars at all. How had we left cell phone reception behind so fast?

I pocketed my phone again, figuring that it wouldn't be very useful on this trip unless I wanted to listen to music I had downloaded, and with Kari so worried about noise I didn't think this would be a good time for that.

We kept walking, and our surroundings got creepier and creepier. The air felt heavy, and it seemed to somehow be thicker as well, absorbing light so that it got hard to see far in any direction. There wasn't any breeze at all, but the trees and branches would still occasionally shift and groan as if in a strong wind. I started to get a strange feeling that the ancient trees all around were watching us, and not in a good way. If you've never run into hostile trees before, I can tell you that it's pretty nerve-wracking.

As a matter of fact, it felt a lot like being at a store and having the security guard decide you're bad news, so he follows you around waiting for you to make a wrong move so he can bust you. I wasn't at all sure what the trees were guarding, but whatever it was I somehow felt pretty certain they were just waiting for me to do the wrong thing so they could drop a hammer on me.

I started to wonder if maybe the trees actually were guards of some kind and we weren't supposed to be walking through this forest. Or maybe we had to stay on some special path that only Kari could see and the trees were waiting to see if I took a wrong turn.

As if unfriendly trees weren't enough to worry about, vague shapes were moving around just far enough away to be lost in the gloom under the huge trees. Every once in a while, one of the shapes would come close enough that I could almost make out the figure of something that somehow seemed really dangerous, but then it would fade back into the murkiness again. After several of these almost-encounters, I heard what sounded like the padding of heavy paws right behind us and jerked around to look backward with my heart racing. But there wasn't anything there that I could see, just the formless shapes in the shadows and those trees watching us.

All right, I know that sounds weird. But those trees were watching us. And I'd had about as much of this as I could take.

"Kari!"

She hadn't looked back in a while, but now she spun around and glared at me. "Liam," she whispered. "I told you we have to be quiet. You are making so much noise as it is—"

"I'm being as quiet as I can!" I hissed back at her.

"You sound like a herd of stampeding trolls!"

"Well, excuse me, Miss Robin Hood, but I never learned how to sneak silently through jolly Sherwood Forest!"

I could tell Kari was getting ready to snap at me again, but she stopped and gave me one of those looks instead. "Why did you call me Robin? And why do you think this forest is named Sherwood?"

"I didn't! I—"

"We have to be as quiet as if we are hunting," Kari insisted. "Move silently or else something will come hunting us."

"Kari, look, I don't know how to walk as quietly as you in the forest. I don't know how to hunt."

"You are joking again." She searched my face, her expression disbelieving. "Almost everyone knows how to hunt, and even those who do not hunt know how to move quietly through the woods so as to avoid any danger stalking them. How could you get to your age without learning those things?"

My mouth opened, but no sound came out. Eventually, I shut it again and glared at her before I finally thought of an answer. "It's not something kids learn in my world. Well, some do, but a whole lot of kids don't."

Kari looked as if she had been hit with a brick. "I do not believe it. Is that why you cannot avoid the ads?"

"I'm sure it has something to do with it. Look, Kari, I know I said I'd come along for this, uh, quest of yours, but you never said anything about basilisks or..." I waved my hand around. "This."

"What?" She gazed around. "Said anything about what?"

"This forest."

"What about it?"

Infuriating. That's the one-word definition of "sister," I decided. How could I admit to her that this place was scaring me when she seemed completely at home? She was worried about the basilisks, true, but since the creatures also terrified me, that wasn't exactly a point to use against her. "Kari, how about we head back home?"

She looked confused. "Your home? Go back to where we started? What would be the reason for that?"

"Safety?"

"That is not a reason!"

"Yes, it is! It's a very good reason."

"But we have a quest to fulfill, Liam. You said you would help."

"You never mentioned basilisks," I repeated. I knew I had her there.

"You are serious." Kari stood facing me, her hands on her hips. "You cannot be serious, but you are. You actually want to quit already."

"No! I just want to, uh, go back that way. Toward home."

"I do not believe it. You are my brother! And we are not even there, yet. We have not confronted any of the challenges—"

"Challenges?"

"I cannot imagine—"

"Hold on," I interrupted. "What's that about challenges?"

She waved one hand dramatically. "Oh, nothing you would care about, I am certain."

"I care about challenges. Are we talking dangerous challenges?"

"They would not be challenges if there was not any danger involved, would they?" Kari demanded.

I shook my head, looking back the way I thought we had come. "That's enough for me. Let's go."

"I am not going back! We cannot afford to waste the time!"

"Well..." This was a problem. I had a pretty strong feeling that if I walked back alone the way we'd come, I wouldn't be able to find home. More likely, whatever was lurking in those shadows would have me for lunch, or I'd step off that special path that might or might not exist and the trees would wallop me big time. "Kari, be reasonable."

"I cannot afford to be what you call reasonable, Liam. I have a job to do! If you will not help, then I will have to do it alone." She turned away.

"Hold on! You said you can't do this alone."

"I will have to," she shot back over her shoulder.

I gave her stiff back the nastiest look I could manage. I was stuck, one way or the other. I was mad enough at the moment that if it hadn't been for my strong suspicions that I couldn't get home in one piece without Kari I would have started walking right then and there.

No matter what you may have heard, I'm not a total idiot. Since I couldn't walk, I started thinking. I had told Mom I would bring Kari back, and I couldn't do that if I let her go off to face some "challenges" on her own. For that matter, I didn't think I could face myself if I let her go on alone now. I mean, we had started this together and I had said I'd help. How could I leave her, sister or not, without feeling like a total loser?

Yeah, maybe it's dumb, but people aren't supposed to leave other people in the lurch. Heroes in the movies don't do that. As a matter of fact, in the movies people who leave other people to fend for themselves usually ended up getting nailed first. But the point was that in stories you don't walk away from someone who needs you. I'd never thought much about applying that in real life, but Kari, annoying as she was, said she needed me.

She needed me to keep our universes from exploding. Maybe getting home shouldn't be my first priority, not if that meant waiting around for everything to blow up, even if my sister was leading me through the Basilisk Haunted Forest of Doom toward The Dangerous But Undefined Challenges.

She was literally leading the way despite any dangers, though. If Kari had been any other girl but my sister I would have been thinking by now that she was pretty hard core. "You're right. You win."

She looked over her shoulder at me. "I win?"

"Yes. You win," I repeated. "Let's go get mauled or eaten or turned into rocks or whatever. Lead on."

Kari twirled about to face me and smiled so brightly the forest gloom seemed to retreat a bit. "I knew you were just jesting with me again! Really, I did. Or were you testing me, to see if I would abandon you once I learned you had not the skills of a hunter? You should have known that would never happen, dearest brother. Whatever the challenges prove to be, we shall face them together!"

Yeah. Great. I'd get mauled with my sister. That'd be a lot better than getting mauled all by myself. Not. "Can you do me a favor, Kari? From now on, could you mention stuff like basilisks *before* we're actually threatened by them?"

"Oh. You were not expecting basilisks?" Kari seemed almost as surprised as when I'd said I couldn't sneak through the woods.

"No."

"Really?"

"Really."

"Very well. I will try to give you warning next time. Do not worry, Liam. The walls between worlds are weak enough that their guardians cannot hinder us *much*... And, after all, having basilisks around is a good thing, in a way."

I gave her a suspicious look. "Why is having giant snakes that can turn us into stone around a good thing?"

"Dragons hate basilisks, as I am certain you know," Kari said cheerfully. "So as long as we are near basilisks, we do not need to worry very much about dragons."

"Dragons?" I took a deep breath. "Kari?"

"Yes?"

"Payback for this is going to be huge."

"Payback?"

"I'll explain later."

Kari started walking again. I tried to move a little quieter this time, but Kari's occasional pained looks back at me told me I wasn't doing a great job.

As we kept walking the gloom started to lift bit by bit, the vague shapes retreated until I couldn't see any more trace of them, and I noticed Kari gradually relaxing. The trees got a little smaller and started to thin out. At some point I stopped feeling like the trees were staring at my back. I began catching glimpses of open meadows ahead, where amazingly green grass shone under a bright sun. Finally, Kari turned to me and waved me up beside her. "That is it. The first challenge is overcome. We are Elsewhere!"

I tried to unknot muscles tensed from waiting for the slithering sounds of giant snakes looking for a couple of snack-size teenagers. "It's safe now?"

"Safe?" Kari asked. "Not exactly. Actually, no."

My muscles tensed up again. "Do we still have to worry about basilisks?"

"Of course not! There are no basilisks in this region, and we will see my friends soon. But traveling in such a small party, just the two of us, exposes us to more peril."

It's funny, but up to that point I hadn't really given any thought to Kari having friends in her nowhere place. She had mentioned that Archimaede thing, but beyond that all I had were mentions of things like unicorns. I hadn't paid too much attention to those because, let's face it, girls are hung up on unicorns. "What are your friends like, Kari?"

"Oh, they are all sorts."

Somehow I didn't doubt that. "Big sorts? With big swords and heavy armor?"

Kari actually laughed. "Not so much of swords and armor, perhaps. But you can depend upon them. They have taken care of me and taught me many important things."

Maybe a half an hour ago I would've made some joke to myself about all the things Kari *hadn't* been taught, but that last half hour had done a lot to shake my confidence that she was clueless and I was clued-in. I had a growing feeling that the shoe was on the other foot now.

Despite Kari's warning, there didn't seem to be anything preparing to eat or massacre us. Instead, the place felt incredibly peaceful. We passed through patches of dappled sunlight, the green grass of the meadows beckoning not far ahead now. Birds were singing and some of them spiraled down to perch on Kari and exchange gossip with her. Aside from the songs of the birds and the sighing of the wind, it was quiet in a way that was almost spooky. I looked up at the sky and all around, slowly realizing that in Kari's Elsewhere I wouldn't hear any motors running nearby or in the distance, no roar of jet aircraft passing overhead, no throbbing of helicopters. No lawn mowers or leaf blowers, no music. I could have hauled out my phone and cranked up some tunes, but somehow that felt totally wrong.

No, this place was quiet in ways I had never experienced. Just the wind and the birds and... "Are those dogs?"

"Wolves!" Kari cried as the pack burst into howls and sped toward us. She had her sword out and was using her free hand to back me toward the nearest tree. "I am sorry, Liam. In my haste to leave your house I forgot to remind you to bring your sword."

"I don't have a sword."

I finally had the satisfaction of seeing Kari's jaw actually drop in amazement. "That is not funny right now, Liam."

"I'm not trying to be funny. I don't have a sword."

I could see Kari watching the wolves advance, swinging her sword lightly before her in short, slow arcs. "But you know how to use a sword, do you not? Of course you do."

"Of course I don't." Kari made some sort of strangled sound, though she kept her eyes on the wolves. "Kari, people in my world don't use swords."

"What an impossible place! Who could imagine such a thing? How do you defend yourselves from packs of wolves such as this?" Kari demanded.

"Well, we could use guns, I guess. But most people don't have them either."

"No wonder your world is overrun with ads! It is your own fault!"

"I can't argue with that." My foot encountered what felt like a good-sized fallen branch and I bent to grab it. To my relief, it turned out to be about the size of a baseball bat. I got a good grip on the base. "This I can use."

Kari stole a sidelong glance and grinned in relief. "That is wonderful. You are not totally helpless."

Put that way, it didn't sound so wonderful.

The wolves were getting pretty close, moving slowly now and spreading out, snarling as they came. They were bigger than I'd thought wolves would be, big enough to trash just about any dog that I knew of that might have tried to take them on. The wolves had matted fur and their snarls revealed big, sharp teeth which didn't seem to have ever been cleaned by a vet. It's funny just how loud a wolf's snarl can sound when you are in an otherwise almost-silent forest. I got a few whiffs of their scent and realized they also stank pretty bad.

If I could've seen any place to run to, I'd have been running at that point. I hoped I wasn't shaking bad enough for Kari to see.

I looked over at her. Kari faced the wolves without a quiver of fear, her face intent, her sword hand steady. "Liam," she whispered, as if trying to avoid letting the wolves hear what she said, "we have had no chance to practice defending each other. Watch my back and I shall watch yours."

"I...I..."

"Do not worry, Liam. You can count on me."

"All right." I didn't tell her I wasn't sure how much she could count on me. I had a definite lack of experience with using an improvised club to fight off wolf packs and I was scared half out of my mind. It occurred to me that I'd told Kari I didn't know how to defend myself using the weapons around here and yet she hadn't hesitated to stand with me and fight. I knew plenty of people who I think would've been all too happy to literally throw me to the wolves while they ran for cover. But the sister I didn't have, the one I'd just met, wasn't going to leave me.

To think I'd tried to walk out on her back in the forest.

"They are about to make their move," Kari whispered again. Her sword was moving very slowly now, its point ready to leap in any direction. I tried to imagine I was in a virtual-reality game where I couldn't really get hurt, hefted my improvised bat, and prepared to see if I could knock a few wolves out of the park.

A big wolf missing half of one ear suddenly leaped straight at Kari. She barely seemed to move her sword, but the wolf flew off to one side, yelping in pain, leaving a red spray of blood arcing through the air in its wake. I caught a blur coming from my left and realized another wolf was leaping at her. Before I could really think about it, my tree branch bat came down and around as I swung with all of my might and connected. The wolf went flying back into the pack, bowling over several of its companions. My hands stung and I almost dropped the branch, but managed to recover my balance and keep my grip.

"Well done," Kari said.

"You, too." I really wished I had a sword. Or maybe a suit of armor. Or an attack helicopter that could lift us out of here.

What I had was a broken tree branch and a girl who thought I could be trusted to watch her back. So I tried to swallow my fear and look menacing. The wolves didn't seem to be fooled, though.

The pack slunk closer and I had a feeling that more than two were getting ready to leap this time. It seemed like a really good moment for the cavalry to arrive.

CHAPTER FOUR

OF UNICORNS AND BEAVERS

HOOVES THUNDERED BEHIND AND TO OUR RIGHT. I HAD A moment to wonder if the cavalry really had arrived, or maybe King Arthur and his knights. I'd be happy either way. The wolves were turning tail and bolting for the deeper woods. Kari raised her sword over her head and started singing something in a language I didn't recognize at all.

The sound of hooves split around the tree we were backed up against, and then I saw unicorns sweeping past on either side. No, I didn't think they were horses at first. If you had seen them you wouldn't have thought that, either.

Before I knew what was happening the wolves were vanishing into the depths of the forest, pursued by a few of the unicorns. The rest of the unicorns slowed to a walk, then turned and came cantering back toward us so gracefully that they seemed to be gliding over the ground, while I stood there with my mouth hanging open and the branch dangling forgotten from one hand.

Kari cheered again, bringing me back to my senses. "Oh, Liam, my friends are here!"

"Your friends?" I took another look. I know meeting a sister you don't have and following her through a haunted forest while worrying about basilisks isn't exactly what you'd call normal, but actually seeing unicorns who had just rescued me from wolves was too much. The day had just reached past some limit in my brain and gotten too strange. "Kari, would you pinch me?"

"What?" She gave me a startled glance. "Pinch you?"

"Yeah. I need somebody to help me make sure I'm not dreaming all this."

"As you wish." Kari returned her sword to its sheath on her back, balled up her fist and punched my arm.

"Ow!" My sister, it turns out, has a wicked punch. "Why'd you do that?"

"You asked me to do that."

"I asked you to pinch me! I didn't ask you to punch me!"

"Pinch, punch. Let us not get too concerned with details, Liam. Did I hurt you?"

"Hurt me?" My little sister? "No! No! You didn't hurt me. You just, uh, surprised me. Yeah. That's it."

"I regret surprising you, Liam. Are you now convinced that you are awake?"

"Yeah, I'm convinced." I took another look at Kari's friends. "I think." Kari raised her fist with a questioning expression. "I'm sure! I'm sure!"

"Good. I cannot wait for you to meet my friends."

I'd seen plenty of pictures of unicorns, but of course I'd never seen a real one. Let me tell you, the pictures don't do them justice. You would figure a unicorn just looks like a horse with a horn stuck on its forehead, but you would be wrong. The unicorn closest to us was amazingly beautiful. Its white hair shimmered as if rainbows were dancing across the surface and every muscle, line, and limb of the unicorn was perfectly proportioned. It was the first time I could think of that I'd seen something I could actually call flawless.

Kari leaned close to me to whisper. "She is named White Lady of Eveness. She is a very important unicorn. I think you would call her the principle unicorn in your world."

The unicorn walked slowly toward us, moving so elegantly that her hooves appeared to part the blades of grass instead of walking on them. She came right up to Kari, putting her muzzle over Kari's shoulder so Kari could hug her neck. When the unicorn drew back, she was smiling. I know. Horses can't smile. Well, unicorns can. Don't ask me how. This one did.

Then she spoke, which normally would've freaked me out, but by that point I'm not sure anything would've surprised me. "Kari, my spirit daughter, it is good to see you."

Kari almost, but not quite, had the same expression she'd had when looking at Mom. "White Lady, it is good to see you! The other world is so strange."

The unicorn tossed her head. "I feared to let you go there. You know that."

"But I had to go, and see whom I have returned with! My own brother!" Kari turned her radiant smile on me, leaving me feeling a little ashamed for the hard time I'd given her earlier.

The unicorn looked at me, but I didn't spot any radiance in her expression. "Yes. So you have." She didn't seem impressed by me at all. "He has agreed to help?"

"Of course! I told you he would."

"He is of there, not here. Do not forget this, daughter." The unicorn rolled one big eye at me. "Why does he not speak to me?"

Kari tried to whisper in the unicorn's ear but I didn't have any trouble hearing her. "I know this sounds strange, but I do not think that Liam has ever met a unicorn before, White Lady."

The unicorn turned its head enough to roll the other eye in my direction. "Well enough, but manners are manners."

Kari looked suddenly embarrassed. "My pardon. The fault is mine. White Lady of Eveness, this is my brother Liam. Liam, this is White Lady of Eveness, who has been like unto a mother to me these fourteen years."

Oh, man. Kari had been raised by a unicorn? That might explain a few things. "Pleased to meet you," I said slowly.

"Are you?" The unicorn walked a couple of steps closer to me, bending her head so that the point of her horn came to rest against my forehead. I realized that all that she had to do was lean forward and I'd be in for a lot of hurt. "I do not know you, Liam, brother of Kari, not as I know your sister."

I swallowed and spoke very carefully. "Yes, but Kari is my sister." At this point, I wasn't about to question that issue.

"So she is." The unicorn raised her head, removing the horn from its resting place uncomfortably near my brain. "Why are you here?"

I pointed at Kari. "Because she made me come here."

"That is not why you are here. Why are you here?"

"She made me come here! Just ask her!"

"Did she put the Sword of Fate to your throat and compel you to march with her?"

"Uh...no. Not exactly."

Kari smiled at me. "Liam often makes jests, White Lady. He is so good at them that sometimes I do not even realize he is jesting!"

The unicorn didn't seem impressed by that, either. "An unusual skill but one of doubtful use. You chose to come here, Liam, brother of Kari. Why?"

"Because..." I gave Kari an angry look, remembering our argument in the woods. Kari just kept smiling, apparently sure this was another one of my jests. "She did make me come here. Not with that sword. But she was coming and if I didn't come along she'd be alone so I had to come, too. She said she needed my help." You'd think a unicorn could understand that.

Well, maybe you wouldn't think a unicorn could understand that. I guess it depends on what you expect from a unicorn.

This one lowered its head enough to tap my forehead again very lightly with that horn. "Liam, brother of Kari, anyone can hold onto things of little value. Such things go nowhere, for no one cares to take them. But to hold onto something of great value requires strength of will and clarity of purpose, to grasp and to hold tightly when all the world seems to be working to take that thing of value from you. Can you so grasp and hold the true treasures of your life, no matter how hard the task?"

It turns out unicorns talk like that a lot. If you ever meet one yourself, you need to remember that, because you've got to be careful how you answer. I learned that, too, later on.

I took a minute to puzzle out what the unicorn had said, and then shrugged. "Yeah. I can do that."

"Think carefully on that answer. Do you speak truth as you know it? Would you vow to live up to it?"

I felt like I was back in school, being quizzed by Mr. Weedle, and not liking it. Maybe I'm a kid, but I'm not a *child*. "Uh, yeah. Yes. I'd vow that."

"Hmmm." The unicorn backed off a step and turned her head to look at Kari. "Daughter, do you truly trust this one?"

Kari gave me that very serious look of hers. "Yes, White Lady."

"He does not seem strong."

"Oh, he is much better than he seems! He guarded me well in his world, warning me of its dangers and bringing me to my honored mother. I do believe he can be trusted."

"Hmmm," the unicorn repeated. "He does not look it."

"He is my brother!"

Who wasn't feeling all that great at the moment. Here I'd tried to walk out on her earlier, and all the time I'd been thinking Kari was weird and brainless because she didn't know much about my world. Okay, I still thought she was weird, but so far I'd turned out to know even less about her world than she'd known about mine. Truth to tell, Kari had been acting suspiciously smart since we'd headed for this Elsewhere place. Her only blind spot seemed to be me, as if she believed the brother she'd never met just had to be the greatest thing going.

On the other hand, the unicorn wasn't pretending to think much of me at all, and until you've been put down by a unicorn you don't know what a put down is. But Kari was standing up for me. The sister I didn't have thought enough of me to argue with a unicorn. You've got to admit that's special. Or maybe unusual. But it's something.

White Lady looked at me. "Kari means much to us all, Liam, brother of Kari."

"Yeah, well, she's *my* sister."

"And what does that mean to you, Liam, brother of Kari?"

What *did* that mean to me? Fighting off a pack of ravenous wolves together had been sort of a bonding experience, but there weren't many wolf packs to worry about in my neighborhood. It was all very well to have Kari giving orders in the Forest of Doom, but I already had enough people ordering me around back home. And Mom had taken Kari's side in an argument five minutes after she walked in the door for the first time! So, I still didn't want her coming home with me and spoiling my perfectly good life.

But I couldn't very well say that while Kari was standing there beaming proudly at her brother and defending me in front of her friends. I'm not perfect, but I'm not that big a jerk.

White Lady was watching me, waiting for an answer to what having Kari as a sister meant to me. "I'm still figuring out what that means," I admitted, which was partly true since I was starting to think that even if Kari never came home with me it might still be okay to have a sister in another world. If I had to have a sister, having her in another world seemed like a good arrangement.

My answer seemed to be the first thing I had said which pleased the unicorn. "I am grateful to have a truth from you rather than glib words, Liam, brother of Kari. You face challenges, and at such times truth to others, and to yourself, means more than any other quality."

Kari nodded. "I am certain that Liam understands that, White Lady. He jests with me on occasion, but in the end he is always true. I have not known him to be false in any way."

It's funny how hearing someone say really nice things about you (when you don't think you really deserve those nice things), can feel a lot worse than having them say bad things about you. I started to wish that Kari would yell at me some more so I could get mad at her again.

One of the other unicorns, a stallion who seemed pretty laid back for a unicorn, nodded his head and horn at me in a friendly way. "Liam, brother of Kari, I am Revek, Bane of Wolves. I saw that you did acquit yourself well against the wolves even though you lacked a sword."

White Lady shook her mane, gave the stallion a look, then focused back on me. "Yes, Revek. He lacked a sword. Where is your sword, Liam, brother of Kari?"

White Lady sure had a way of focusing on uncomfortable details. This seemed like a bad time to admit I didn't have a sword, but I opened my mouth even though I had no idea what I was going to say. Before I could say anything, Kari grabbed my arm and started talking. "His sword was taken from him by the evil Lady Meyer of Hillcrest."

A murmur of surprise went through the herd and the stallion blurted out, "Taken?"

"Yes!" Kari insisted. "By a ruse, just as she succeeded in temporarily taking the Sword of Fate from me." Another murmur of surprise, mingled this time with outrage. "She asks to see the blade, with false courtesy, then attempts to keep it for her own. And after she takes their swords, the evil Lady Meyer suspends her victims!"

"Suspends?" Revek gasped. "That sounds ill."

"Yes," Kari agreed, "though Liam spared me the details while we were in his world."

Everyone looked at me, expecting some comment, so I nodded quickly. "Yes. Being suspended is a bad thing. It's the pits."

"The pits!" Revek shook his head in disbelief. "This woman suspends her victims over pits! Say no more, Liam, brother of Kari."

White Lady hadn't stopped looking at me. "And yet Kari managed to recover *her* sword."

Kari jumped to my defense again. "He selflessly aided me in escaping the grim fortress of Hillcrest, and then in recovering the Sword of Fate instead of seeking his own blade."

Did Kari really believe that was what had happened at my school, or was she deliberately putting things in a way that would make me look best to her friends? Maybe she was doing the same thing here that she had done when we faced the wolves, guarding my back and counting on me to guard hers when she needed it, even though I couldn't think of anything much I'd done to make her believe I was all that great a guard. Strange as it seemed, I was starting to wonder if maybe Kari figured that her brother naturally deserved that kind of support.

As for me, I was beginning to wonder just what I had ever done to deserve that kind of loyalty from anyone, let alone a sister I had never met before today. Maybe I ought to think about trying to repay that loyalty. Annoying or not, Kari seemed like a decent kid, and she had been real nice to have around when the wolves were after us. "I'm here to help Kari," I said. "And I'll do whatever I can, I'll fight however I can, whether I have a sword or not."

"Well spoken," Revek applauded. I was liking that unicorn stallion more every minute. "I only regret that when all is set right here we will not be able to assist you in rendering justice to the evil Lady Meyer of Hillcrest."

Kari raised one fist. "Liam and I shall bring her to bay! She will rue the day she embarked on her path of repression! Her rule shall be ended, the gates of Hillcrest shall be flung open, its dungeon emptied and her victims set free to live in peace and joy!"

I was starting to worry about what would happen in the unlikely event we both did end up back in my world and Kari ended up enrolled in my school. I mean, I was still sure that wouldn't happen, but what if it did? It didn't seem too likely that she and the evil Lady, that is, Principal Meyer would be getting along very well. Especially if they tried to make Kari sit down filling out circles on standardized tests crammed with whatever trivia we had been force fed to produce better standardized test results. If that didn't make much sense to me, who had grown up with it, I couldn't see Kari just accepting it.

No. From what I had seen of her so far, it was way too easy to imagine Kari doing a Joan-of-Arc thing and leading an army of students in a siege of the teachers' lounge. Home schooling. That would be the ticket for Kari. Mom wouldn't mind once I explained the alternative.

If Kari did come back with me, which she wouldn't. Right? Who would leave a herd of unicorns in a beautiful place like this to live in the suburbs? She would stay here, and I would go home to be the only kid in the family again. Win-win.

But now White Lady swung her head again to point with her horn across the meadow. "The Archimaede awaits, Kari. It tells us time grows short, but we cannot assist you from this point onward. You must hasten and the two of you must do so alone."

Kari gracefully went to one knee, bowing her head toward the unicorn. "My eyes and my heart joy to this meeting and sorrow in this parting. Grant us your well wishes on our journey, White Lady of Eveness."

If a unicorn can be said to have a tender expression on her face, White Lady did as she looked at Kari. "You shall always have those wishes with you, my spirit daughter, no matter where you must go."

"But—" Kari's voice choked for a moment. "If I must never see you again—"

"The choice is not ours or yours, daughter of my heart. Return in time and we may hope for farewells before you leave forever."

Leave forever? No, that couldn't mean, like, *leave*. As in leave this Elsewhere place. They had to be talking about Kari leaving these unicorns and going somewhere else in Elsewhere. Yeah. Because they obviously didn't have phones or chat here, so moving somewhere else would mean not being able to talk to each other all the time anymore. Which was why they sounded so sad.

But what if it did mean Kari was leaving as in *leaving*? Where would she go? Home with me? No. That's obviously not going to happen because...

What if she is? What if I have to share the rest of my life with a sister? A sister who was raised by unicorns?

No. Won't happen. Can't happen!

The unicorn White Lady looked at me and I didn't get any tender vibes at all. I once again got the uncomfortable feeling that she was reading my thoughts. "I send my heart with you, Liam, brother of Kari, for your keeping, though I sense little welcome in you for her. Know this. Fail her, and you shall fail yourself as well."

I wasn't sure how to answer that, and I was unnerved by White Lady figuring out how I felt about Kari, and I was pretty sure that if I tried to do Kari's kneeling thing I'd fall over and look like an ultra-maroon, so I tried to bow to the unicorn. All I could think to say was, "I'll do my best," which doesn't really mean anything, but usually sounds good. I followed as Kari stood up and began jogging across the meadow in the direction White Lady had indicated. The unicorns all stayed behind. When I glanced back I saw them standing, watching us.

Kari didn't say anything, lost in thought, so I stayed quiet as well while we crossed the meadow, concentrating on my breathing as I matched her pace. It wasn't easy, even though she was weighed down with that sword and I wasn't. Kari would be a shoo-in for the track team at Hillcrest.

I had to watch my feet as we ran through the high grass, but I caught glimpses of the wider world as we ran. Vast mountains rearing up to one side, an ocean or some other big body of water occasionally visible some ways to the other side, and up ahead a small river that gleamed in the sun. Everything seemed impossibly bright and sharp, which I suppose is how things are when there's not a lot of pollution in the air. Birds chirped and swung by, their colors so brilliant they almost hurt my eyes, but Kari waved them off, her face still somber. Aside from the rhythmic sounds of our breathing, the only noises I could hear were our feet swishing through the grass and an occasional sharp cry of what sounded like a hawk overhead.

Finally, just when I was about to admit I needed to rest, Kari slowed to a walk. I stumbled to a walk as well, trying to keep from collapsing in the grass.

"Forgive me," Kari said in a low voice punctuated by long, slow breaths brought on by the run. "I am somewhat saddened, as you see."

"Um, yeah," I managed to gasp back to her while I tried to catch my breath. I never claimed to be good at talking about feelings. I'm a guy. Besides, there hadn't really been anyone to discuss feelings with. But, for some reason, seeing Kari depressed like this bothered me. I mean, why should it bother me? I didn't know her. Did I? Maybe she was growing on me. It was increasingly obvious that Kari was tough as nails as well as good with her sword, and she had this irrational belief that I was something special. As sisters go, that wasn't a bad combination.

Kari sighed again. "I shall miss this world."

Miss this world? Oh, man. "Um...why don't you stay?" I managed to get out between wheezing for breath.

She looked away. "There is only one choice."

Talk her out of it. Hurry! "Because of Mom? She'd be disappointed, I guess, if you stayed here, but once I told her about White Lady and how much you liked it here—"

"You do not understand. I am grateful that you are trying to help, but you do not understand."

The girl could not take a hint. "Really, Kari, if you *want* to stay—"

"My *wants* are not the issue! I cannot think of myself!"

"Why not? I mean, seriously, what's wrong with focusing on what you want?"

She turned to stare at me. "This is an ill time for a jest, my brother."

"But if you don't *want* to come stay at my home, I wouldn't *mind*—"

Kari shook her head. "It is nice that you care for me enough to want the best for me, but it cannot be."

I hoped that she didn't notice my flinch when Kari said that bit about my caring for her. How could someone saying you were good make you feel so bad?

This was going to ruin everything. Why had I only now confirmed that she was definitely planning on coming home with me once our quest was over? Okay, maybe I should've cleared that up a little earlier. I suppose you think that you'd have done a better job of managing things if the sister you didn't have showed up at your school with an enchanted sword and roped you into a bunch of challenges in another world.

Fortunately, Kari was absorbed in her own thoughts and didn't notice the emotions that must have been showing on my face. I didn't know how I could have explained them without hurting her more, and she already looked really unhappy.

I tried to think through my life to understand how she must feel, and kept ending up with big blanks. Sure, I'd had a few disappointments, but only on the scale of not getting a certain video game for my birthday or not getting to go to a party. Had I ever missed out on anything really important? Had to give up anything really important? I glanced over at Kari, remembering the way Mom had looked at her. Shocked and stunned and upset, but also...also happy. I'd seen that. I hadn't wanted to admit it. "Kari? Mom is really going to be happy if...I mean, when you come home."

I'd said it. *When you come home.* My life was officially over.

She smiled a little. "Thank you, Liam. I must remember that in the other world I will still be among those who love me." Then she balled her hand in a fist and rapped my shoulder again, much more gently this time, clearly including me among those who she thought loved her.

Oh, man. I looked away and shrugged, hoping she wouldn't see through me, feeling like a total jerk. "You're, uh, not so bad. Sometimes."

"'Not so bad'? This is a compliment in your world?"

"Sort of."

"Then you are sometimes not so bad yourself, Liam," Kari repeated solemnly. She pointed to where the river bank met the meadow not far ahead. "The Archimaede awaits."

I followed Kari as she worked her way down the river bank and toward what looked for all the world like a huge beaver house. In front of the beaver house sat what looked for all the world like a huge beaver, its head easily six feet off the ground, holding a branch in one hand as it chewed on the wood.

I was still looking around for the Archimaede when Kari ran the last several steps and into the embrace of the giant beaver. "Archimaede, I have brought my brother."

I caught up just as the Archimaede switched its gaze to me. Its eyes were big and deep and very definitely not those of just any ordinary giant beaver. "It is well." It had a deep and mellow voice, just about how you'd expect a giant beaver to talk, if one ever did talk.

I stood awkwardly for a moment while Kari snuggled against the Archimaede's fur. Feeling ridiculous to be talking to a giant beaver, I gave a small wave. "Uh, hi."

If there was some special greeting for Archimaedes, the creature didn't insist on it. "Your name, brother of Kari?"

"Liam." I realized something that was starting to bug me. All of my life I'd been the only child, the only kid point of reference in my family. The Eagan kid. Now, to all of these people I was just "brother of Kari." It felt funny. I wasn't sure I liked it. My feelings toward Kari and this whole mess kept ping-ponging around and leaving me more confused than ever.

The Archimaede waved toward a nearby log. "Come sit with us, Liam, brother of Kari. There is much to discuss and too little time."

I wasn't too comfortable getting within reach of a giant beaver, but Kari obviously wasn't worried, so I sat down on the big log not far from her and the Archimaede. It eyed me appraisingly before speaking again. "Did Kari explain the task before you?"

"Yeah. She said something about a quest. We have to get some objects from my world that are here and return them where they belong."

"Just so. There are three things which must be returned to your world. You must find two of them."

"You've already got the third?" Finally, some good news.

The Archimaede pointed to Kari. "Your sister is the third."

I felt a sudden lump in my guts as I turned to look at Kari, who had that my-world-is-over expression on her face.

"Yes," she said sadly, head bowed, looking at the sand. "I must return. If I stay, the walls may not heal, and it was my presence here which helped draw the other two objects. If I stay, the crisis will repeat in time. And so I must go."

I stared at her, suddenly understanding. She didn't *want* to come home with me. No one was *making* her come home with me. She *had* to. She had to leave the only home she had ever known, a really cool place where she could LARP for real full time, and go to a new place where the most she could hope for was going to school at the grim fortress of the evil Lady Meyer. "Kari, I...I'm sorry. I didn't realize... That's just awful. It's really, really awful."

She nodded, trying to smile even though I could see some tears welling in her eyes, and that made me feel even worse. "It will not be so bad, dearest brother. As you reminded me, Mother is there, and you will be there."

Yeah. Great. I'd be there. Me with my welcoming attitude. My perspective flipped for a moment, and for the first time I didn't see things as me having to have Kari move in, but rather saw myself as Kari, having to move in with me. And let me tell you, I felt even more sorry for Kari then. "Um...yeah," I mumbled.

"Liam, brother of Kari," the Archimaede said, drawing my attention to him. "Do not judge how well or how poorly you have completed a journey before you take your first steps."

How had he known what I was feeling? "I know who I am."

"Do you?" the Archimaede asked. "Few really know themselves, and even then they see truth only in fragments. You have come this far, through the walls between worlds, and that is not an easy journey."

I perked up a little. Yeah. I had done that. I'd wanted to walk out on Kari, but I hadn't. Still, the last thing I wanted to talk about was me, because at the moment I wasn't too impressed with myself. Time to change the subject. "Speaking of the walls between worlds, I was wondering about those trees in that weird forest."

"They're not really trees." The Archimaede gazed thoughtfully at the actual trees not far distant. "What you saw were the guardians of the walls between the worlds, though the word guardian itself implies an intelligent purpose which may not be accurate. Your mind could not grasp the reality of the guardians, those things which normally prevent any passage between worlds, but your senses could not accept their true form, and so you saw and felt what you could understand."

"Then, they're imaginary?"

"No," the Archimaede corrected firmly. "They are very real. It is the form which you saw which is not true. But they are deadly and powerful even when weakened. Do not mistake that." He sighed, a great gust of wind coming from him. "And they are weaker than I had calculated. We have much less time than I expected. I had thought the danger would grow steadily, but the stress on the walls between your world and this one is increasing along an ever-steeper curve."

I could understand that. "It's, what, a logarithmic progression?"

"Exactly!" The Archimaede beamed at me, then his whiskers drooped in sorrow. "My calculations were in error. Kari, you could not have traveled to find your brother before this because the walls had not weakened enough, but now we must find those objects *today*. By the time the sun sets, the damage may be too great to repair."

Kari looked up at the sun. "Are they far?"

"Not too much so. The objects were drawn to you, and so came to rest not far from here. I can tell you in general where they lie. It is not an impossible task, but you will have little time for leisure."

Her sorrow replaced by determination, Kari nodded. "Then Liam and I will succeed."

"Wait." The Archimaede chewed on its branch for a moment. "There is something else you must know. The other two objects must be found. But that is not all. I have run my calculations and read the probabilities. In order to have a chance of succeeding in this quest, Liam, brother of Kari, must also fulfill the three promises he has made this day."

"Excuse me?" I looked at Kari, then back at the Archimaede. "Three promises? I didn't make any promises."

"Oh, but you did," the Archimaede insisted. "Three, as I said."

"I don't remember making any promises!" I know I'd said some stuff to the unicorn, but I couldn't remember the words "I promise" anywhere in there. Not right now, anyway. And I couldn't believe that I'd somehow managed to make *three* promises during my brief conversation with White Lady or with anyone else. "What were they?"

"I can't tell you," the Archimaede said.

"You can't tell me? I have to keep three promises and you won't tell me what they are? What kind of deal is that?"

"The only 'deal' there is, I'm afraid. I don't know what the promises are. I know only that their existence has altered the possible path of events today. Even if I did know exactly what they were, telling you would skew the probabilities in all the wrong directions and perhaps doom your quest."

"What does that mean?" I demanded.

The Archimaede gave me what must have been intended as a reassuring smile, though coming from a giant beaver that involved way too many huge, sharp teeth. "In simpler terms, by telling you what you should do, I would cause you to act differently. Anything I tell you will change what you do, most probably for the worse. Your quest will have the highest chance of success if you make your own decisions."

Great. For years I've been pushing Mom and Dad to let me make my own decisions, and now I get just that from a giant beaver with the fate of the universe, no, *two* universes, hanging in the balance. "You've got a lot more confidence in me and my judgment than most people do."

The Archimaede bowed slightly toward me. "The confidence must be yours. Trust in yourself."

"Look, if there's one thing I've learned," I said, "it's that confidence doesn't do the job. In order to win, you also need to know the rules. If you know the rules, how things work, you can figure out the loopholes and the tricks."

"There is truth to that," the Archimaede mused.

"Then if you know anything else, you have to tell me what it is, and you have to tell me the rules. That's only fair."

"No," the Archimaede said. "I don't have to tell you any more, even if I could. I didn't create the situation we're dealing with, Liam, brother of Kari, but I can assure you that whether or not you consider it fair is of no consequence. Surely you understand the most basic rule of all, that the universe isn't very big on the idea of fair."

"You can't make me keep three promises when I don't even know what they are!" I said.

The Archimaede sighed again. "I can't make you do anything. Only you can decide what to do. In any case, you made the promises, not me."

"I think I'd remember making promises!"

"Perhaps you make promises of great import too lightly, Liam, brother of Kari," the Archimaede suggested. "Perhaps you promise without thinking, even though a promise is among the most valuable of possessions for anyone who keeps them, and among the most worthless of things for those who do not."

I slumped back, shaking my head. "This sounds like one of those martial arts movies where the hero is supposed to learn the secrets of life while polishing the sensei's car."

I got another very toothy grin. "I don't have a car, whatever that is, and I don't have time to teach you anything. Whatever you need to succeed must be within you already."

All right, then. We were toast. Two entire universes were going to be toast. Because all this giant beaver could tell me was that life wasn't fair, and I didn't need a giant beaver to tell me that. "I guess I shouldn't have bothered worrying about that book report that's due tomorrow."

The Archimaede shook his head. "You may yet fail your book report."

"That's something to look forward to."

"Liam, Kari's fate as well as your own will depend upon it. While I don't have any particular feelings for you, I do care a great deal for this girl, whom I have taught for season upon season. Can you try for her sake?"

Unfair. Really, really unfair. Kari gave me a brave look, and I realized that I couldn't just leave her to explode along with everything else in two universes. The crazy girl trusted me. "Yeah. I'll give it my best shot."

The Archimaede chewed a little more, watching me in a manner that reminded me uncomfortably of the way the unicorn White Lady had looked at me. "Do you have a Teacher, Liam brother of Kari?"

The way the Archimaede said it, I had no trouble hearing the capital T in Teacher. I had to think about that. I had a lot of teachers, but did I have any Teachers? Somebody who taught more than the stuff that they ask you to know for standardized tests?

Kari spoke up helpfully. "Perhaps the kwan-tum you have mentioned, Liam?"

"Uh, no." I looked into the Archimaede's eyes and then I knew the answer. As a matter of fact, I felt a bit ashamed that I'd had to think about the answer. "Dad."

Another big, giant-beaver grin. "Your father?"

"Yeah. He's taught me stuff that isn't in any book."

"That is well, for he will be Kari's father, too. I may send her forth with that consolation. And Kari's mother? Is she a Teacher as well?"

"Well…" I was about to say "she's just Mom" again, then remembered how White Lady had looked at me when she was sizing me up. That unicorn had the same look in its eyes then as Mom did when she was interrogating me about my life. "She's like White Lady, sometimes, I guess."

"Mothers tend to be the same in certain ways, don't they?" the Archimaede said. "Then Kari shall be well looked after if you should both reach your home again."

"If? Aren't you supposed to be giving me a pep talk here?"

"There are many possibilities and no certainties. I never lie, Liam, brother of Kari. Exactly which dangers manifest themselves is impossible to predict with any certainty, exactly what you will do cannot be predicted, and so I can only offer uncertainty."

"Feel free to lie! Tell me we're going to win!"

Kari smiled at me. "There will be no danger we cannot overcome together, dearest brother. We do not need the Archimaede to tell us that we shall succeed."

All right. If I couldn't get some foolish hope from anyone else, I'd accept it from the sister I didn't have. Of course, *she* wasn't worried. Because she was nuts. I was pretty certain of that by now. Even more nuts than most sisters, as far as I could tell. But I'd played enough quest games on my computer. I knew what happened when a party of adventurers started out. They got waxed. Again and again. That's what saved games are for. And clue books.

I was still trying to retrace my steps since this morning in a vain attempt to figure out how I'd gone from English class to facing death under orders from a giant beaver with the fate of two universes riding on my ability to make the right decisions, when the Archimaede reached out and touched Kari's hand. "I will miss you, She Who Is Apart."

The strange phrase at least distracted me from wondering how many possible dangers awaited us. I watched Kari and the Archimaede looking at each other and it held my attention because it reminded me of something. Dad and I used to do that, didn't we? Sometimes, I guess. I vaguely remembered once thinking he could do no wrong, back when I was just a little kid. But he'd changed. Or maybe I'd changed. Did we ever look at each other like we'd used to, now? Or did what Kari had called being blinded by familiarity also keep me from really seeing my dad anymore? "Can you at least tell me one thing?" I asked. "How did Kari end up here instead of in my world?"

The Archimaede nodded. "Yes, I can tell you that. Kari came to us on a wave of probability which slipped through the walls between worlds. The tiny possibility that would become Kari was to be there. Instead, in a moment of immense improbability, she was here."

At least he had finally answered one of my questions. "A probability wave? And Kari talked about her wave function once. That is quantum physics."

Instead of reflecting Kari's ignorance of the term, the Archimaede shrugged, which is a very strange gesture to see in a giant beaver. "Your world uses the words quantum physics to explain much that you don't yet really understand. In time, more understanding will come to you. Then you may call it something else. The name matters less than the meaning."

Kari nodded as if she had understood every word. "Then you do know Liam's kwan-tum, Archimaede?"

"Certainly. If fate brings you to the home of Liam, brother of Kari, again, you will find much of what I taught you of use there."

"Wait a minute," I interrupted. "This doesn't make sense. I'm old enough to know kids don't come from storks or probability waves."

The Archimaede nodded again. "True. Kari's actual arrival in this world came in the form of a considerable surprise for a certain noble elven lady. When Kari was born the fact that she was fully human was an even greater surprise, though at least it proved the lady's claims of innocence in the matter to the satisfaction of the elven royal court. They brought her to me, and after I explained to them what must have happened, I took her to White Lady."

"Huh? Why didn't the elves raise her?" That happened in stories all the time. I looked at Kari, saw that she was staring at the ground with a very rigid set to her face, and wished that I'd kept my big mouth shut.

"It's a bit complicated," the Archimaede advised me in a gentle voice. "Elves, especially elven ladies, do not mix with humans here. There is a vast gulf dividing the emotions and ways of thought of elven-kind from human. Far better for Kari that she be raised by one who could give her love."

I just nodded back instead of saying something else stupid.

The Archimaede took the piece of wood out of its mouth and used it to point toward that big ocean I'd caught glimpses of. "The objects that cause the stress in the walls between worlds lie that way. I cannot see them clearly, but listen well. One of the objects holds time frozen behind walls of stone. It is in that direction. The other belongs to no world and rests in the well of the fire. It is farther to the east, and more distant."

"Huh?" I said. "I thought these objects were from my world."

"They are."

"Then how can the second one belong to no world?"

"I don't know, Liam, brother of Kari. You must find it and determine what that means."

Great. "Is anything today going to be simple?"

The Archimaede caught my eyes with his own. "You may find some of the decisions you must make to be simple ones, Liam, brother of Kari. Following them may not be simple, but you will know what you must do."

I nodded wearily. "Like fulfilling three promises I don't' remember making."

The Archimaede nodded back at me. "Do remember this, if you seek reasons to do what you know in your heart to be right. If you don't fulfill the three promises, I'm afraid the chances of your getting home again are very, very small indeed."

"That's a good reason to try. A very good reason. And if I do carry out these three promises I'll get home and everything won't explode?"

Another shrug. "Hopefully. There are few certainties in life."

"I know it isn't going to make any difference, but I'm still going to tell you that that's not fair!"

"The universe doesn't make promises, Liam, brother of Kari. People make promises. By so doing, they bind themselves, but they also create the conditions under which they can change the universe. Magnificent, is it not?"

"Magnificent isn't quite the word I'm thinking of."

Kari stood up, one hand reaching up and back over her shoulder to grip her sword by the hilt even though she kept it sheathed. "Do the objects we seek have guardians?"

"Very likely, yes," the Archimaede said, "though they probably know not what they guard. Bring the objects back to me, Kari. Before the sun sets."

Kari had already started in the direction the Archimaede had pointed but stopped when I spoke again. "If we're not back by sunset, the game's over?"

The Archimaede hesitated, then nodded. "I believe so."

"Okay. See you before sunset, big guy." I figured if I was stuck in a game with no clear way out and a lot of stuff to get through before I won (if I survived), I might as well get into the mood for it just like Kari. I could go just as Conan, or Red Sonya, as she could. Well, except that she had a sword and I didn't.

But I didn't bother asking about the guardians as Kari and I left the Archimaede. I figured either he wouldn't tell me, or he would tell me and I'd wish he hadn't. It may take me a little while, but sooner or later I do figure out some of the rules.

Chapter Five

We Have Always Lived in the Castle

THIS WHOLE THING WASN'T TURNING OUT TO BE MUCH FUN after all. Instead of enjoying a stroll through a park inhabited by friendly elves I was being chased by wolves, put down by unicorns, and lectured to by giant beavers who set ridiculous deadlines. I couldn't recall that sort of thing happening to any of the heroes in any of my books or games. Aside from the wolf part, that is.

Worst of all, there were real consequences if I failed.

At least remembering my games got me thinking about how the characters always started out weak and grew into major heroes as they gained experience. Maybe that would work for me here. It's not like I had any chance of turning into Conan the teenage barbarian before sunset, but I could learn enough to maybe keep from being a happy meal on two feet for the next pack of wolves we encountered. Because if it was all about figuring out the tricks you needed to survive, I knew how to do that from my games. You just needed to keep cool, don't do anything dumb, and keep trying different things. I only had to hope I didn't make any major mistakes along the way.

Not that I had a lot of time available to learn in, if the Archimaede was to be believed. Only until sunset. Just how long did that give us, anyway? Right now, Kari was walking along with a quick, wide stride that ate up distance and left me wishing I'd worked out harder during PhysEd class. I had no way of knowing if we should be hurrying faster or if we had time to slow down and maybe search for some food, because my stomach was very unhappy with the fact that lunch time seemed to have arrived with nothing but some long drinks from the stream the Archimaede lived along.

I pulled out my cell, which seemed to be working fine aside from no bars and no service. If my cell was to be trusted, it was about half past twelve now, but the sun here appeared to still be rising and nobody had mentioned lunch yet. Did time work the same way here? Were the days were the same length? "Is it already noon, Kari?"

She glanced at me. "No. The sun is yet a palm's width short of its highest point."

That didn't help much. "How long are the days here?"

"In this season, the days are longer than the nights."

"Kari, my cell says it's twelve thirty—"

"Says?" Kari asked. "I heard nothing."

She couldn't be serious. Could she? "I mean," I said with what I thought was great patience, "according to the time on my phone, it's twelve thirty."

"Twelve and thirty? What does that mean?" Either Kari was a great actor, or she really had no idea what I was talking about.

Maybe if I tried another approach. After all, what mattered was how much time we had left. "When does the sun set, Kari?"

Kari frowned at me. "Are you serious?"

"Yeah. It's a simple question, isn't it?"

"Very. The sun sets when the sun goes beneath the horizon," she said.

Obviously my sister had decided to get difficult again. "And what time is that?"

That got me another frown. "In the evening. At sunset."

"Can you be a little more specific?" She just stared at me. "Like the hour? Five o'clock? Six o'clock?"

"Hour? O'clock?" she repeated, as if she had no idea what the word meant.

"Yes!" I held up my cell. "What time is it on your phone or your watch when the sun sets?"

Kari shook her head. "Phone? Watch? You mean that thing of yours?"

"You don't have a watch? You can't tell time?"

I hadn't meant to needle Kari, in fact I was too stunned to be picking on her, but her face got red and angry. "I can mark the passage of time, Liam! I am not an infant. I can watch the shadows shorten and lengthen, I can measure the span of daylight and I can read the seasons. Cannot tell time! I do not need a silly piece of jewelry to tell me the sun is high but still short of the nooning!"

I guess she had a point. "Sorry. I didn't mean...that is, in my world we use stuff to tell us exactly what time it is, so I could tell you the sun would set in, like, five more hours."

"Why would that matter?"

"It would tell us how much time we had left!"

"We have until sunset," she said, as if repeating something obvious.

I had to take a moment to calm down before I tried explaining again. "Look, if we knew that we had, say, five hours left, we'd know how much time we had to get this stuff done."

Kari frowned up at the sky. "But we already know that we have until sunset."

"How do we know when half that time is gone?"

She raised one arm and swung it across the sky. "When the sun has fallen halfway toward setting from where it is now, of course."

That was way too simple and way too sloppy. "But if we knew the sun was going to set at—" I stopped, trying to think. What time *was* the sun setting these days? I hadn't really been paying attention. I mean, why bother when you can just flick on a light and keep doing whatever you're doing? "You know what's really weird? I can tell you the time down to the exact second, but I can't tell you even within an hour when the sun sets at this time of year. I just don't notice. How's that for strange?"

Kari seemed ready to make some comment, but stopped herself.

"But you don't even know what hours are," I continued, "and you probably have a much better idea than I do of how long we've got until sunset. How could knowing more mean that I understand less?"

"The Archimaede calls that a paradox," Kari said. "But he also says that almost every paradox is imaginary, that if you adjust your own way of seeing things you will understand that what you think is impossible is actually just the result of how you are thinking about it."

"You mean a paradox like me not having a sister but her showing up to haul me off on a quest?"

"Something like that."

I didn't answer for a while, taking the Archimaede's advice and thinking about it. "The Archimaede really is pretty smart, isn't he? Now that I think about it, I don't even know if you use daylight savings time here, so whatever time I thought it was might be off anyway."

This time Kari looked surprised, as well as impressed. "You can save daylight in your world? How is this done?"

"Uh...we don't really save daylight. We just call it that."

"Why do you call it saving daylight when you aren't saving daylight?"

"We take some time from the morning and put it in the evening."

"You move the sun?" she asked skeptically. "And then put it back later?"

"No. The sun stays where it is, but we just say that's a different place."

"And this gives you more sunlight during the day?"

"No," I said. "It just moves the sunlight around."

Kari gave me a look like she was trying to figure out if this was another jest. "Why? Do people in your world enjoy pretending to move the sun?"

"Um...I don't know why. It's not because we enjoy it. Nobody I know seems to like daylight savings time." This time I frowned as I looked ahead. "You know, there's a lot of things like that in my world. Things we do even though nobody really likes them and they don't really make sense, but we have to do them anyway, maybe because we've always done them. Like daylight savings time and the qwerty keyboard and irregular verbs."

Kari nodded as if she actually understood me this time. "Customs usually are created for a good reason, but will often continue long after the reasons for them no longer exist. White Lady told me that. The unicorns still meet with the Elven court once a year in the Spring, because at one time unicorns and elves fought together to stop the yearly incursions of ogres. The ogres ceased coming long years ago, though no one knows why, yet the meetings continue." She looked troubled, and stopped talking quickly.

Having already messed up once talking about elves and Kari, I decided to drop that. "Let's start over. I was just wondering how much time we had to finish this quest thing."

Kari pointed at the sun. "Until sunset."

"I mean *exactly* how much time!"

"You mean in these hours of yours? What difference would knowing that make?" Kari asked. "We are already pursuing our quest as quickly as we can. Would you work any slower if we knew how many of these hours we had before sunset?"

"Well, yeah. Of course. Why rush if you have plenty of time? We could pace ourselves. You know. We could take it a little easier and still get done before the deadline."

Kari screwed up her face in bafflement. "How could you judge that we had plenty of time? In order to know that we would have to know all possible obstacles and all possible hindrances and how much distance we must cover and what unpredictable things we might encounter!"

"Yeah, but, if we knew that stuff and we knew how much time we had..." My voice trailed off as I realized how dumb that sounded.

"We do not know those things," Kari pointed out.

"Yeah." Forgive me for trying to think things out. Though I knew I was really mad because she was right. I didn't like Kari being right and I didn't like having a deadline so close but being unable to measure that deadline. I didn't like having to rush like crazy toward some "guardians" because we couldn't tell how much time we had to think stuff through beforehand.

And let's face it, I was getting worried. I was used to knowing details, knowing what I had to do and how long it would take and what I could get away with and how long I could put off doing it until I had to. But now I was in a situation where I didn't know any of that.

If Kari had doubts like mine, she didn't show any signs of them. But since we had left the Archimaede she had been alert and serious in a way I was starting to recognize. When Kari wasn't worried she did the annoyingly cheerful bit, but when danger threatened she got real business-like. I wasn't sure whether I should be comforted by the fact that she was taking things seriously or scared about whatever danger had her worried.

Now she sped up a little more, her eyes fixed on a point ahead of us where some sort of structure had become visible. I walked faster, too, determined not to let on that I was having trouble keeping up. Whatever she was looking at was too far off for me to make out anything but the fact that it was sort of blocky and pointy. "What is that?" I asked.

"It is a castle," Kari replied immediately.

"A castle? Cool. Who lives there?"

She shook her head. "I have no idea."

"You've never been there?"

"I have never even seen it before," Kari said.

I looked back the way we had come. "We haven't come that far from where the Archimaede is. How come you've never been to this castle? Don't the unicorns or the Archimaede ever talk about it?"

Kari shook her head again. "It was not here," she explained. "It has not been here. Now it is here."

"Castles just appear out of nowhere?" I asked.

"No." She gave me another one of those quizzical looks. "The castle had to have come from somewhere. I do not know where. But it could not have been nowhere, because then it would not exist somewhere."

"Oh, yeah, right," I said, as if all of that made sense. Maybe it did make sense, though. Or maybe rules don't have to make sense as long as everyone understands what they are. Sort of like daylight savings time. The rules here might be different, but there were still rules.

Kari continued talking. "Things appear in Elsewhere. Then they leave, then they appear again, somewhere else. Some things stay the same, but others do not. Does everything stay the same in your world?"

I thought of buildings being torn down and replaced, and new houses being built everywhere you looked. "Not exactly. Sometimes it seems like you just turn around and there's a house standing where there were only trees before."

"Yes." Kari nodded. "Just like here."

I didn't think it was all that much "just like here," but didn't see any sense in arguing about that. "How do you even know it's a castle, then? Can you actually see that well from here?"

"No. My bird friends told me." She gestured forward. "I asked some of them to scout the castle for us. They should be back soon to let us know who lives there."

I'd noticed her chirping and singing to passing birds as we walked, and had tried to ignore it. But maybe Kari's ability to talk to birds wasn't simply annoying and weird. Maybe it could actually be useful. Before I could say anything else, three birds came swooping in close, one landing on Kari's offered arm to twitter and tweet. She tweeted back, then the bird leaped into the air again while Kari walked on, her expression troubled.

"They say the castle is uninhabited," Kari reported.

"Nobody's there?"

"Nobody and nothing," Kari corrected. "They saw nothing living at all."

I didn't want to ask the obvious question, but figured I had to know the answer. "Did they see anything dead?"

"No."

That was a relief. Unless something had killed *and* eaten everything. "Do you have any idea why a castle would be uninhabited?" I could think of various reasons and didn't like any of them.

"The birds say they could not see anything to account for it. It is not a large castle, but it is surrounded by something odd. They could not explain it to me."

An abandoned castle surrounded by something odd. Just my idea of a great place to visit. "Isn't that sort of strange? That the birds can't explain it?"

Kari shook her head again. "Not at all. There are many things in the world that birds have trouble understanding. Like windows."

"Windows?"

"Yes. It looks like an open arch, and sometimes it is, but other times there is an invisible wall across it. Glass. It simply baffles the birds." She looked over and caught my expression. "It is not because they are dumb, you know. It is just something outside of their experience."

I almost laughed at Kari's defense of her bird friends, then remembered our little walk through the woods to get to this place. I still had no idea how Kari had done that. Definitely something outside of *my* experience. Until today, that is. "That's a good point," I finally agreed. "So, is there a reason why we're walking toward that mysteriously deserted castle with something odd around it?"

"One of the objects which we seek must be there," she replied confidently. "The Archimaede said we should seek it in this direction, and that it lay behind walls of stone. Well, you see the walls of stone, and they are in the right direction. Nothing lies beyond the castle but the Great Sea, and if the object lies in the Great Sea we shall face serious troubles indeed in recovering it."

I mumbled something about getting travel directions from giant beavers.

"What was that, dearest brother?"

"Nothing. Nothing."

Kari glanced up at the sun and started going even faster, pushing our pace, even though I felt a lot more like hanging back and waiting to see if any nasty guardians showed themselves. As we got closer, we could make out the outlines of the castle better, and see that it rested on a rocky bluff which fell away toward the sea. The far side of the castle walls must be right on the edge of the cliff. Despite my skepticism about scouting reports from birds, I couldn't see any sign of life either as those gray stone walls loomed higher and higher before us. A couple of pennants hung totally limp from the tops of towers even though I could feel a fair breeze blowing in from the water, as if the wind itself refused to visit the abandoned castle.

It gave me the creeps. This appeared to be exactly the sort of place where in the movies the teenagers' car breaks down and they have to seek refuge for the night and then they all meet horrible fates one by one until nobody's left but the Smart Girl who figures out how to narrowly survive. Kari would obviously fill the smart girl role, since I was reluctantly concluding that she was sort of smart even if she was also crazy. That left no room for me, the smart-aleck, self-absorbed kid, at the end of the story.

Not only was I beginning to regret watching movies like that, but I also didn't like my growing realization that I would be the smart-aleck, self-absorbed character. Not the hero, but the guy whose painful death made the audience applaud.

Some more birds flew down and perched on Kari, chirping frantically. She gave them a soothing song back and then released them once more into the air. "They are worried," she confided to me in a whisper.

"So am I," I whispered back at her.

She smiled as if she thought I was kidding. By this time, we were both jogging. I started to wonder if Kari planned on just running into the castle, but she finally slowed to a walk again when we were a short way from the castle's gate. Loosening her sword in its sheath, she scanned the battlements in a careful way that made me feel a little better. Kari looked so competent at times like that, like she knew exactly how to handle things. She might be annoying and crazy, but she also knew what she was doing when dealing with stuff in this world.

We walked right up to the moat without seeing any signs of life inside the castle. The drawbridge was down, the portcullis raised, and the gate open. "Sure. It's always easy to get into places like this," I complained. "Getting out is another thing."

Kari smiled. "I admire your ability to jest at such a time," she said.

I'm not sure why, maybe because I was still trying to catch my breath from our jog, but I followed Kari without protest as she strode into the castle. Our footsteps boomed across the drawbridge, echoing from the dry moat below. I expected the portcullis to slam down and the gate to slam shut once we'd walked into the castle courtyard, but they didn't move.

Nothing moved.

The courtyard wasn't all that big or all that impressive. Stone walks led here and there, but between them was nothing but bare dirt that wasn't broken by even a single dead weed. A few wooden tools, a wheelbarrow laying on its side, and an empty, horse-drawn wagon without its horse were scattered about. I couldn't feel even the slightest breath of wind. Between the totally still air and the sun beating down the courtyard felt unbearably hot and stuffy, so that even though we were in the brightly lit outdoors it seemed strangely like being in a room that had been completely sealed up. In front of us, the circular keep rose skyward, a tower of stone pocked with empty windows.

Kari looked around, searching every window and doorway. "I see nothing, Liam." Her voice should have echoed in that empty space, but it didn't. The sound just sort of got sucked out of the air.

"I don't either." I spoke louder than I'd intended, but the sound of my voice didn't go very far before it disappeared, too.

"We'll have to look inside."

Of course. That would be where the impossible-to-stop bad guy was waiting. I wanted to debate this "have to" stuff with Kari, but since I had no desire at all to stay in that courtyard alone I followed her as she walked up the broad steps leading into the castle's central keep.

Nothing jumped out at us. The inside of the keep felt as motionless as the outside of the castle. Kari kept going, searching deeper into the keep, while I tried to think of some excuse that would get her to lead us out of that place. It was obvious to me by now that being raised by unicorns doesn't do much for common-sense in sisters, especially this particular sister, so I couldn't appeal to her on those grounds. Every second I was regretting a little more having followed Kari on this quest, but it's funny how being in a deserted castle that reeks of some hidden danger will make you want to stick close to even the weirdest relative. I stayed right with Kari as we walked through the first and second levels of the keep at a rapid pace, one eye out for monsters and one eye out for some object from my world.

Here and there we could see personal items lying about, none of them from my world unfortunately. The furniture and tapes-tries inside the keep seemed undisturbed by time, intruders, or weather. "Where is everybody?" I finally demanded, wanting to hear at least the sound of my own voice again in that silent keep even if it might tip off something bad that we were around.

Kari shook her head. "It is very disturbing, isn't it?"

"Yeah. Disturbing."

"It doesn't look like they left, but they are gone."

"Maybe we ought to leave before we're gone, too."

Instead of agreeing with what I thought was a pretty intelligent suggestion, she kept on searching. "Have you seen an item from your world yet?" Kari asked. "One where time is held frozen?"

"No and no. Believe me, I'd have told you if I had. I'm not even sure what 'where time is held frozen' means."

"Then freezing time isn't something usually done in your world? Or is it like your saving of daylight?"

I bit back my first response, remembering that someone who thought it was perfectly normal for castles to appear out of nowhere might not think freezing time was all that impossible. "Freezing time usually only happens in math classes. Those can last forever."

She eyed me warily for a moment. "That is one of your jests, isn't it?"

"Right."

"That's good, because I haven't seen any signs of mathematical instruction in—" Kari stopped speaking, staring around, one hand on her sword hilt. "Can you feel it?"

"Feel...?"

"Hush. Hold still."

Given the circumstances, I didn't have any problem with following her orders this time. So I stopped and tried to feel. And somehow I did. It wasn't just the air. Something was drawing the life from this place. Something that wasn't too far away. I know this doesn't make any sense, but it felt like watching water drain out of a sink, only there wasn't any sink or water and I couldn't see anything, but I could tell life was draining away into... something. "That's it. I'm out of here."

"This is no time for more jesting, brother."

"I'm not jesting, Kari. I'm deadly serious."

"Good. We must face this threat with great care."

"That's not what I—"

"I feel it there." She pointed toward the far side of the keep, then nodded to one side. "I will go around this way. You go that way. If it attempts to flee, we'll have it trapped."

"*We'll* have *it* trapped?"

"Courage, Liam!"

"Brains, Kari!"

She actually laughed softly as if I were joking. Then her face went serious again and she began cautiously moving in the direction she had chosen.

I barely managed to overcome the urge to grab something and throw it at her. Talk about someone only hearing what they want to hear. Why on earth did Kari think I'd want to hang around some monster that sucked life out of castles, let alone try to catch the thing?

I guess this was the downside of Kari thinking her brother was such a great guy. She apparently expected me to live up to it. I felt a lot more like running away, but in the movies the guy who tries to run away from his friends always runs right into the monster and dies first. Besides, I've never liked the guys who did that. But standing around here waiting while the thing maybe snuck up on me didn't seem like a good idea, either.

Which meant my safest option was to do what Kari said. Rats. Mentally throwing up my hands in exasperation, I tried to very carefully and quietly move in the direction Kari had pointed.

It wasn't too long before I lost sight of Kari, but the keep wasn't that big around so I knew I'd see her soon. I went cautiously from one piece of furniture to the next, trying to stay both hidden and protected as best I could, not even breathing loudly while I listened and watched with all my might. Okay, I was at least a quarter of the way around the keep now. I'd see Kari real soon. Or I'd hear her fighting whatever that thing was and have to decide which direction I should run.

No Kari. No monster. No noises. I kept going, even as I started to get a nasty feeling that I was more than half way around the keep. But maybe I was mistaken. I went further. Still no Kari. Then I recognized a piece of furniture. I'd come all the way around the keep and hadn't seen her.

Which could only mean it, whatever *it* was, had Kari.

Running away was now obviously the smart thing to do. If Kari, with her sword and her skills suited to this nowhere, could get snapped up without a sound, what chance did I have trapped in an abandoned castle and not a cheat code in sight? I turned toward the stairs down, but found my feet wouldn't move.

I hadn't seen any blood or stuff, so Kari was probably still alive. And there was only one person around who could help her.

Unfortunately for her, that was me, and no matter what Kari might think I was no hero. I couldn't even move my feet to run away.

I looked back the way she'd gone, thinking of Kari in the hands of some monster. I tried to take a step in that direction and this time my feet moved.

Stupid feet.

I'd gone completely around once and not even seen anything, let alone been attacked. It wouldn't hurt to walk around again, would it?

Maybe.

I did anyway.

Perhaps it was because I wasn't expecting to see Kari any second this time, but I felt that life-sucking feeling more strongly as I worked my way back around. Then, to my surprise, I felt it diminish a little. As if it'd moved away. Or as if I'd passed it...

I walked back a few steps, paused, then forward a few steps, trying to figure out at what point the feeling got strongest.

Eventually I found myself looking at a mirror.

A big mirror, taller than me and wider, too. It had been mounted on the outer wall somehow, so that it looked into the center of the keep. The frame was some sort of dull metal that looked like no amount of effort could ever make it shine. At one time there had apparently been some kind of decorations on the metal, but whatever had been there was so worn down that all I could see were misshapen lumps on the frame. Something in the back of my head was grateful that I couldn't make out any of the old decorations, as if some sixth sense of mine somehow knew they would have been really unpleasant to look at.

I peered into the old mirror, seeing the slightly wavy reflections of everything out here. Except that, oddly enough, none of the colors from out here were reflected in the mirror. In the reflection, everything looked gray, like in one of those old movies.

Then I spotted the reflections of people. Gasping, I whirled around, and saw nothing. Nobody there. I tried to get my heart back to beating normally and looked into the mirror again. There were definitely people reflected, scattered around here and there within the mirrored castle.

I know vampires don't reflect in mirrors. That's, like, common knowledge. But reflections without people? I reached out to rub at one of the reflections, and felt my finger sinking slowly into the mirror.

Yikes. I pulled my hand back, staring at my finger which seemed none the worse for wear. Let's see. Kari had come this way. Kari had disappeared. There were people in that mirror, and apparently a way to get into it. Therefore, Kari must be inside that mirror. If Kari was inside that mirror, she might need help. No, let's face it. She definitely needed help, or I'd have heard from her already.

All right. I'd found out where she was. Now I could go get help. Some of those unicorns. It would only take...hours. What if Kari needed help right now? What if this castle disappeared again while I was gone? And even if everything worked right I had a feeling it would be sunset by the time I had retraced our steps, rounded up a posse, and made it back.

No saved games here, Liam. No way to try one thing and see what happens, then go back and try something else. I only got one shot at making the right decision.

That thing might be waiting right inside the mirror. Or Kari could be fighting for her life right now while I stood here. Did I want to spend the rest of my life knowing I had left Kari to some monster because I was too afraid to even find out if she needed me? Me, the guy who liked to imagine he would have taken the ring to Mordor?

Okay. I'd do it. I fought down my fear of the unknown, put my hand flat against the mirror, and pushed, watching my hand and arm disappear into it. There wasn't much resistance once I'd gotten started. Before I knew it, or had time to panic, my head and body were going through.

I guess I was expecting some wild burst of color and bizarre, computer-generated imagery, but there were no exciting special effects. No menacing soundtrack, either. If I hadn't been so scared I would have been seriously annoyed by the lack of chrome in this situation.

I stepped out of the mirror and it looked like I was inside the castle. No, wait. Everything was on the opposite side and the only colors I could see were on my skin and clothing. I was in.

Do you know how you can look into the edge of a mirror and it just seems to go on and on, as if the entire world were somehow reflected in that one mirror and you could see it if you could just get past that edge? That's what it was like inside the mirror. As far as I could tell, the entire castle was "reflected" in here, and I caught glimpses of the outside world through the windows. But everything was colorless, just drab shades of gray.

I still didn't see Kari. I also couldn't see any monsters. What I could see much better now were what I had thought were reflections of people, but now seemed to be statues, scattered here and there around the place. With visions of basilisks and Medusas dancing in my head, I snuck toward one of the statues to see if it looked a little too real.

It did, with details in the clothes and face that I didn't think any sculptor could have achieved. Oddly enough, though, the face on the statue didn't show any sign of fear. I figured if I saw a monster I'd probably have time to look really unhappy before I got the stone treatment. This person, though, didn't betray any expression, any emotion, just eyes and a face that appeared to have gone lifeless even before they turned into stone. All the statues were like that. If you've ever been in a school assembly with the most boring speaker in the world, you'd understand how all those statue people looked, like they'd been listening for what felt like forever and had given up hope of ever hearing or seeing anything interesting ever again.

If Kari was in here, I needed to find her before she or I or both of us ended up as part of the floor decorations. I started sneaking carefully through the mirror keep just as I had done in the real keep.

This time I found her, about halfway around, but Kari didn't move when I whispered her name. When I got closer, I could tell why. Her entire body, from hair to boots, had turned a light gray color. Kari's face had that same lifeless emptiness I had seen on the others here.

My stomach suddenly felt like I had swallowed a rock. Why was I feeling so upset at losing a crazy sister I didn't even have until this morning?

Staring at Kari, turned gray all over and her face all sad-beyond-sad, I realized I had actually started to like her a little. It had been kind of fun having her around. Sometimes. When she wasn't being too, you know, strange.

Bring her back, Mom had said, and I had said sure. Because as far as I knew none of my friends had ever had their sisters turn into statues in a deserted castle in another world and have to wonder how they would get her home. Sorry, Mom, there was this mirror and some kind of monster. Somehow I don't think Mom would understand. Yeah, the birds could still perch on Kari, even though she was a statue, but it wouldn't be the same.

I reached out to touch Kari's shoulder, wondering whether it would feel like stone. My fingers came in contact...and I found myself a few feet away, lying on the floor, my ears ringing and my eyes blinking against a flash of light.

That sort of thing never happened to me before when I'd touched a girl on the shoulder, and I was pretty certain that even touching your sister wouldn't knock you halfway across the room. This was definitely unusual.

Then I remembered the flash of light. I'd heard a firefighter describe what would happen if you touched a high-voltage electrical line. This seemed to have been something like that, only it hadn't felt life threatening, just pure pain. I stared at Kari, shaking the after-effects out of my head, and spotted what I swore was a small patch of color on her shoulder about where my fingers must have touched.

Hey, had I grounded out the magic or whatever had turned Kari into a statue? Drained a little of it out of her? If I had, it didn't amount to much. Even as I looked the little area with color faded out and turned gray again.

I sat up and looked at Kari more closely. She wasn't as dark gray as the others here, so maybe she could still be reached. One thing for sure, I couldn't just drop things now without trying something else.

I stood up, crossed my fingers, and carefully stepped closer to Kari again. I reached, hesitated, reached, hesitated, reached....

This was ridiculous. Count to three. One. Two. Three. Grab her shoulder tight.

I held on for a few seconds while my brains got fried, until my grip failed and I went flying backward again. It took a minute for the room to stop going around in circles and the flashes in my eyes to fade before I was able to look at Kari again.

Her shoulder had color. No question. Her shirt looked like cloth. Part of her hair resting near there looked like hair again. But even as I watched the color began to recede under a tide of gray. Within a short time, everything was colorless and Kari was a statue-girl again.

Oh, man. I could tell where this was leading. I knew what I had to do. But how could I? Every time I touched Kari it felt like all of her unicorn friends had started jumping up and down on my head, sticking their horns in my guts, and kicking my legs. Forget it. Game over. I couldn't even hold on to her long enough to make a difference.

Wait a minute. Hold on to her. I get it. That thing White Lady had said. She had made me vow to hold on to Kari, hadn't she? I hadn't known I would have to literally hold on to her while pain danced on me, but I *had* said I would do it.

Yeah, right. I had told a *unicorn* I'd do it. Give me a break. How could that count? Especially since the unicorn had said I wasn't "strong" enough to be trusted. Huh!

Hey.

Okay, maybe I'm not some big hero, but I had walked through that blasted mirror even though I had no idea what was waiting for me. I'm stronger than that unicorn thought I could be. I'd handled fear of the unknown. Now all I had to do was handle fear of the known, because I knew it would hurt like crazy, to help Kari.

Kari, who had told those unicorns what a great guy I was. Who had told White Lady I was a lot stronger than I looked. And I'd told Kari and White Lady they could count on me.

Me and my big mouth. I took another look at that empty face of hers, somehow incredibly sad even though it didn't show any emotion. "Okay! Fine! I just hope you appreciate this, you little pain in the neck!"

Without letting myself think about it anymore, I spread my arms wide, swung them around Kari's waist, locked my hands together and tried to concentrate on holding on.

I couldn't see anything but flashing lights, my ears were full of a crackling, roaring sound, and big fire ants were swarming over me and taking bites inside and out. It just went on and on and I tried to keep my hands holding tight to each other and then it got kind of dark.

"Liam! Liam!"

I blinked. My head felt like I'd been kicked by a mule. Not that I've ever actually been kicked by a mule, but it felt like how I thought that would feel. And it doesn't feel good. Not at all. Kari's voice seemed far away, but getting closer.

"Liam! Let go of me!"

"No," I mumbled. "Going to hold on."

"What are you talking about? Let go of me, Liam!"

I finally managed to get my eyes working right again. I was lying on the cold stones of the mirror castle floor, my arms still locked around Kari's waist. Holding tight to my sister's waist... "Hey! Get off!" I broke my grip even though my hands were numb and scrambled away.

"What were you doing?" Kari demanded. "Hugging me like that?"

"Well, excuse me! I just went through all that and you're giving me a hard time?"

"All what? What did you just go through?"

"You don't know? You don't remember?"

"Remember what?" Kari waved one hand around and looked worried. "I can't remember anything! I was looking in the mirror and then...then I was here on the floor and you wouldn't let go of me!"

"You didn't feel anything? No pain?"

"No."

This was So Totally Not Fair. I got the demon fire ant treatment and Kari didn't feel a thing.

But then Kari's expression changed, and she stared at me with her eyes getting really wide. "I didn't feel anything, Liam. I *couldn't* feel anything. I remember that, now. I could see and hear, but nothing I saw or heard mattered. Do you know where I was?"

"No." I was still feeling more than a little put out over things.

"I was in a place where all dreams are dead, Liam."

Something about her voice pulled me out of my sulk. Kari looked truly haunted by the memory. "Um, well, you're not there anymore."

"How did I get out?" Her face brightened. "Did you rescue me?"

"Uh, I guess so."

"That's why you were holding on to me?"

"Yeah."

"Oh, dearest brother, thank you. You don't know...was it hard?"

"Well..." Was it hard? Of course it was hard. Kari would never know how hard. I should tell her. In great detail.

Or should I? Why tell her? She would never know how bad it had felt unless she went through it herself. Why, then? To make myself look good? Like I was some kind of hero when I had almost walked out of here and left her, when I had been scared to death of doing what any half-way decent guy would have done?

How important was it that she know what I had gone through to rescue her? Or was it more important that *I* knew what I had gone through? And that I had succeeded?

Next time a unicorn accused me of not being strong enough, I wouldn't let it bother me, just you see. I knew better now.

I shrugged. "It wasn't that bad."

Kari looked at me with that very serious face for a moment. "If you say so."

"Hey." I was trying to be the stoic hero here and I didn't want her ruining it by acting sorry for me. "I said it wasn't that bad."

"And I said if you say so," Kari replied in a less sympathetic voice.

"If you don't believe me—"

"Who said I don't believe you?" Kari demanded.

"You did," I shot back.

"I said 'if you say so.' I know what I said."

"That's the same thing!"

"No, it's not!"

"Yes, it is!"

"Why don't you just admit you're wrong?" she yelled.

I started to yell at back at her, then hesitated. "Wrong about what?"

Kari hesitated as well, then frowned. "I am not sure. Whatever it is, we can fight about it again later when we remember and then you can admit you were wrong."

"How can you be sure I'm wrong when we can't even remember what we're arguing about?"

"I just am!" Kari stood up, looking around, and gave a little shudder. "This is an awful place. Not as bad as the place where all dreams are dead, but bad enough because it leads to that place."

"Can we get out?" I was thinking of the monster again and wondering if it had heard us while we argued about whatever we had been arguing about.

"I don't know. Do you know where you came in?"

"Yeah." I came to my feet, too, feeling a little wobbly. Kari gave me a concerned look and I tried to stand steady. "I'm fine."

"I didn't say anything."

"I didn't say you did." I know a little while ago I had been thinking that sometimes it was nice to have a sister around, but this didn't seem to be one of those times. I led Kari back the way I had come.

Kari stared at the statues we passed. "I would be like them if not for you," she finally said. "You do not have to tell me again. Did I thank you?"

"I think so."

"You are a wonderful brother and a trustworthy companion."

"Uh huh." Good thing Kari didn't know how close I had come to bolting out of this tower and leaving her to an eternity of nothing. Well, not an eternity, I guess, since the universe would blow up tonight or tomorrow, but still.

Kari put a wounded expression on her face at my reply though.

"And you're a wonderful sister," I felt like I had to say.

She smiled. Talk about mood swings.

We came to where the mirror of the mirror stood. Inside it, we could see the gray-washed but still clearly colorful world outside. I pushed against it, but nothing happened this time. Same for Kari.

"We have to get out," I suggested, hoping for once she would listen to me. "Before the monster finds us."

Kari gave me a surprised look. "It already has."

I jumped backward, looking around frantically and giving a good imitation of how Kari had reacted to hearing my home was full of invisible ads. "Where? Where is it?"

She pointed at the mirror. "Right here. This is what creates this world. This is what devours all of life's meaning in here."

"That's it?" I came forward cautiously, watching the mirror. "Is it alive? Is it intelligent?"

Kari frowned in thought, shaking her head. "I doubt it. There is no feeling of purpose to it, only the knowledge of its task. It does what it has been made to do, you see?"

That reassured me a little. "Somebody made it?"

"Somebody or something," Kari assured me. "Long ago. Whatever was bound into the mirror is ancient. Those the mirror was aimed at must have crumbled to dust long ago, yet it continues, because it knows only what it must do. *Why* never mattered to it."

"It's like a weapon?" I asked, staring at the mirror.

"Yes. Just so. A weapon that continues to work mindlessly. It is surely much older than this castle."

I came a little closer, peering at the worn engravings and once again being thankful that I couldn't make out what they had once been. "Then why would this mirror be here? I mean, there?"

"Those who lived in the castle doubtless felt the desire to have it near them," Kari explained.

"Doubtless? Why would they have wanted this ugly thing in their castle?"

Kari had been studying the mirror, but now jerked her head over to look at me. "Did you not feel attracted to it?" she asked me with a surprised expression.

"Nooooo. I only went near it because it felt like the thing that was sucking life." Even though it was pretty stupid right now, I had to rephrase that statement when it offered such a great opening. "This mirror sucks!"

"It does," Kari agreed, not getting the joke at all. "You already said that. But your reaction is interesting." Kari looked from me to the mirror and back again. "I felt a strong drawing to the mirror, a need to be close, yet so subtle that I did not realize it was being forced upon me from outside until it was too late. The others here must have been lured inside in the same fashion. I feel it again now. The mirror realizes I have escaped the fate it bound me to, though it does not know how. It is...puzzled."

"You can understand this thing?" I asked, seriously creeped out.

"I can sense its feelings," Kari explained. "After so many years, it has encountered something new, and it does not know how to deal with it." She turned a surprised look on me. "You confuse it. It does not understand you."

"Neither does Mom," I said, "but how does that help us?"

"It has not learned how to counter you," Kari said. "The mirror's lure does not work on you. It has not been able to force you into that place where there are no dreams. But it is trying to figure out how to do that, how to do to you what it did to me and these others."

That last sentence gave me a sinking sensation. Kari had seemed so confident about the mirror that I had been assuming she knew how to defeat it. I had a growing worry that if we stayed inside the mirror for much longer Kari would start going gray again, and I really didn't want to suffer through another rescue. "Let's not give it time to do that. The Archimaede never taught you how to escape when you're trapped in a mirror?"

"Not exactly, but he did teach me how to analyze problems." Kari examined the thing carefully, looking at it from all sides, then stood back to gaze at the mirror, her chin resting on one fist as she thought. Finally, she turned to me. "There is great strength in this object, though I feel that its strength has faded with time. The dark enchantments once adorning the frame have been worn beyond recognition and no longer have any power. That which is bound into the mirror and traps us here is still too strong to defeat in a contest of pure will, however. Therefore, I can think of only one thing to do."

"What?" I kept my eyes on her, since I had learned to worry about the sort of things Kari regarded as reasonable courses of action.

"We must break the ancient spell holding that which is bound within the mirror."

"We must?" That seemed to make sense. At least, it made as much sense as anything else that I had run into today. "How do we do that?"

"By physically confronting the evil in this mirror with the strength of my own spirit."

That didn't sound quite as sensible. "How do you do that?"

"Like this." Kari reached up and back and drew her sword, then reversed it so the hilt was forward. The great blue sapphire on the end of the hilt glowed like a star in the gray mirror-world around us. I suppose I was expecting her to start some magical chant or something. Instead, raising the weapon and bracing herself in a fighting stance, Kari slammed the jewel against the mirror before I could get my horrified yell out of my throat.

Chapter Six

Girls and Boys

THE MIRROR CRACKED UNDER THE BLOW. A VERY DEEP and very loud bell-tone boomed through the world around us. I flinched, clapping my hands over my ears, then almost fell as the entire mirror-world castle shuddered and shifted as if a big earthquake had hit. Ignoring all that, her face determined, Kari drew back her sword and slammed the sapphire against the mirror again.

The cracks spread on the mirror, and as they did much bigger cracks suddenly appeared in the castle around us. The whole structure seemed ready to collapse, dust falling on us, as the shifting stone groaned like a creature in pain.

"Three times breaks the charm!" Kari cried, slamming the jewel on the end of her sword hilt against the mirror a third time.

The mirror shattered, shards flying off in all directions.

I flung out my arms to protect my face as walls and ceiling of stone fell around us. The mirror-castle floor dropped out from beneath me as the structure collapsed into ruin.

I felt a moment of pure panic, then my feet thudded onto a solid surface again with no more force than if I had dropped a few inches. I lowered my arms, wondering what I would see.

And found myself standing back in the outside world again, facing the broken mirror. Kari glanced at the shards, then at the undamaged jewel in her sword hilt, then at me, and grinned. "The spell is broken, that bound within the mirror freed. It has returned into the nothingness from which it was once summoned. My plan worked."

"Good thing," I said, trying to calm down as my body slowly realized that I wasn't about to be crushed in a huge pile of rock. "What if it hadn't?"

"But it did." Kari expertly spun the sword around in one hand and slid it into its sheath on her back with a melodramatic flourish. Show off. I guess she had earned it, though. "There is thought and there is action. The Archimaede teaches that both are needed. Do not act without thinking and do not think without acting. So he says and so we did. We thought the problem through, then we acted."

There was that "we" stuff again. Even though I couldn't fault Kari's logic, I was about to protest that I hadn't been given any vote on the action. But before I could speak again we both heard sounds and looked around.

The keep behind us was full of other people, blinking and staring at each other and us as if they were waking from a long, deep sleep. I recognized one of them. "Hey. He was in the mirror."

"They all were," Kari said softly. "We freed them when we destroyed the thing."

It finally hit me that I had done something pretty cool. Faced the unknown monster, saved my sister, and did it despite my fears and a nasty dose of pain. And that had saved these other people, too. "Yeah!" I raised both arms in triumph. "I'm bad!"

Kari's eyes widened again, but this time in surprise. "Liam! You have done nothing bad. Your actions were good."

"That's what I meant. When I said 'I'm bad' it meant 'I'm good.'"

"How can saying you are bad mean you are good?"

"It's a different kind of bad. It's..." I saw the expression on Kari's face. "Complicated, I guess."

Kari shook her head. "I see," she said in a way that sounded like she didn't see at all. "Very well, Liam. I must say your world is a very strange place."

"My world is strange?" I thought about abandoned castles appearing on the sea shore and dream-sucking mirrors. But Kari apparently thought that sort of thing was perfectly normal. "I guess it depends on what you're used to."

Kari pointed to where the sun's rays slanted in through a nearby window. "We spent a fair time trapped within that mirror.

Having defeated the guardian, we must now redouble our search for the item it guarded, and swiftly."

But when we turned to do that we were confronted by the newly freed prisoners of the mirror. I felt a moment of panic, seeing how many there were, and how many of them had either swords or daggers at their belts. What if this were the accursed tower of a dark ruler who had been caught in his (or her) own mirror trap?

None of them looked like orcs, though. As far as I knew, bad guys always had orcs working for them. And all of them were smiling at us.

One, a woman more richly dressed than the others, stepped forward. "You freed us from the spell of the mirror?"

Kari inclined her head toward the woman. "Yes. I am Kari, Spirit Daughter of White Lady of Eveness, and this is Liam, my Steadfast Brother."

"She Who Is Apart? The elven-born daughter of the unicorn!" the woman cried, then to my surprise she knelt before Kari, and so did the other people. "You have grown much beyond the toddling child I last heard you to be. We must have been enchanted unchanging in that accursed mirror for a ten of years at least. We cannot thank you enough for freeing us from the mirror and destroying the evil which empowered it. I am Lady Amelia Dudley, ruler of this keep. If there is anything we can do to repay you, any gift we can give you, just say it and it shall be yours."

"Rise, Lady Amelia and your followers," Kari said as if people knelt before her all the time. "Fortune and a quest led us here. Your thanks are reward enough. We ask only your leave and assistance in searching this keep for an object from my brother's world."

Lady Amelia got up, nodding to me and not betraying any sign of being startled to hear that I was from a different world. "Certainly. But may I add that in addition to my other treasures, I have a daughter of marriageable age, who would be honored beyond measure to be matched with a hero of the stature of Liam the Steadfast."

Whoa. Apparently this ruler thought I was also of marriageable age.

Kari gave me a sidelong look as she answered the ruler of the keep. "We are honored by your offer, Lady Amelia, but must hasten with our task lest disaster befall all our lands."

Lady Amelia bowed in return. "As you say, Lady, so shall it be. Everyone, harken to these heroes and to what object they seek." As she waved her hand to emphasize her words, the sleeve on her arm fell back, revealing an object that looked suspiciously familiar to me.

"Excuse me," I asked. "Are you wearing a wristwatch?"

The ruler looked down at her wrist. "My bracelet? What did you call it? It was given to me by those who found it. Since then I have worn it as a charm since it seemed a work of great skill and portent."

Kari stared. "Is that an object from your world, Liam? A watch like those you spoke of which holds hours within it?"

"It measures hours," I corrected, walking closer to the ruler and examining the watch on her wrist. "But it's a lot nicer than any watch I ever had. This is one of those really cool ones that are mega-expensive. Not one of those cheap plastic digital jobs they give out in cereal boxes." Everyone was giving me blank stares. "You know, it's bling." More blank stares. "Yes, it's an object from my world."

Lady Amelia removed the watch, then offered it to me. "If you desire it, you may have it. Scant luck has it brought me, and I owe you all I have for freeing me and my people from the mirror's spell."

I took the watch and tried to wave away the praise. "Kari's the one who broke the mirror."

"I could have done nothing had you not saved me first," she insisted. "You have been the means to save all here, and to remove an evil from this world."

Okay, I'm not one to brag on myself but I think I had a right to feel pretty good about that, so I didn't feel too embarrassed by Kari's praise. Plus, we had one of the objects now. I held it up to Kari. "Everything was frozen in that mirror. The watch tells time. Frozen time. One down, one to go."

She grinned and held up both arms in the same triumphant gesture I had used.

Lady Amelia, who seemed pretty cool, wanted to hold a celebration right then and there, but we begged off on the grounds that we had to save the world before sunset and time was flying. I thought the newly freed people took the news that the universe might end after sunset rather calmly, but they were probably still a little out of it from their long sleep. They escorted us to the gate, cheering as we left the castle. This time we could feel the breeze blowing through the stone structure, and see it whipping around the pennants on the towers. Birds were tentatively swooping in, warbling when they saw Kari, as we walked out through the gate and across the drawbridge. Kari and I turned to wave to the people on the battlements as we headed away from the castle. What do you know? Instead of a horror movie ending, we had a happy ending. Funny what you can do if you don't let the bad movies you've seen spook you. "Not a bad day's work," I remarked.

"Our work this day is not done," Kari reminded me. She had started walking fast again, angling out over the fields slightly inland from the coast. "The well of fire we seek must lie in this direction from what the Archimaede said." She pointed, swinging her arm across the horizon. "The coast curves inward up ahead, so we shall tend more to the north."

I looked outward across the fields and woods and felt my heart sinking and my feet starting to hurt. Between our walk through the Forest of Doom and the trip from the Archimaede to the castle, we had already done quite a bit of hiking today. "How do we know the well of fire isn't in the water? Some island or underwater volcano?" Not that I wanted to swim long distances, but maybe there would be an enchanted boat or something we could ride in.

Kari shook her head. "There are no islands within the gulf. I know of no underwater volcano, but if we go so far as to near the coast again we can watch for signs of such and see if any mer-people respond to a hail for information."

"Mer-people?" I perked up a little at that. "Like, mermaids?"

"Yes, there are females, of course." She frowned at me. "Why does it matter?"

"Well, mermaids, they're like, you know."

"I do not know."

"They're...beautiful," I said, feeling lame. "Really hot babes."

Kari's eyebrow rose, then she suddenly laughed. "Do you think they are fair? Liam, they are fish creatures." She mimed having huge eyes and bulging cheeks with gills at the back. "If you find that so attractive, perhaps they will like you, too, you being of marriageable age," she added with a grin.

"Hey, I never expressed interest in that." Though I wished I could have seen Lady Amelia's daughter that I had turned down. Just, you know, out of curiosity. "Believe me, Mom wouldn't have been happy if I had come home with a bride. She was freaked out enough when I came home with a sister. Lady Amelia was serious?"

"In offering you the hand of her daughter? And all the rest of her besides, which I know a man would count of greater interest," Kari added with a laugh. "Of course, Lady Amelia was serious. But do not be overmuch impressed by her generosity. For her daughter to be wed to my brother would cause Lady Amelia to be linked by family ties to White Lady and her realm. You may be sure that Lady Amelia had that outcome foremost in her mind."

"You mean it was just politics? She didn't care what kind of guy I was? She would have made her daughter marry any guy who was related to White Lady if the guy agreed?"

"Just so," Kari said.

I had read about that kind of thing a lot in fantasies and histories, and I've heard that there are still places in my world where girls are forced to marry guys, but I had never had it shoved in my face before. "That sucks."

Kari canted her head as she gave me a questioning look. "Like the mirror? You think it is evil?"

"Of course I do! Girls should decide for themselves who they marry!"

"What if this girl had been beautiful, Liam? Young and lovely, and the man who married her would become heir to Lady Amelia's keep?"

That made me hesitate, which I don't like admitting to, but it did. I mean, some really hot babe who would be mine for the asking? Teenage boys, of which I happen to be one, dream about that kind of thing.

But then I thought of that girl, of her not being mine because she wanted it but because she was being forced to, and that just felt so rotten. I couldn't do that, even if she had looked like some manga babe. At least, I hoped I could never do that.

And, honestly, it felt kind of good to know I felt that way. "No. I still wouldn't be part of a deal like that."

Kari smiled and punched my shoulder again, which kind of hurt since I was still sore there. "I knew my brother would be a worthy man."

I felt my face getting warm from embarrassment, but Kari pretended like she hadn't noticed anything and instead pointed inland. "I think it unlikely the place we seek is surrounded by water. The Archimaede said the other object will be in the well of fire. He gave no indication water was also a feature."

"So you pretty much know what the well of the fire means?" I asked.

"Not for certain. No."

"Couldn't the Archimaede just tell us stuff instead of giving us vague riddles?"

"I do not think so. His knowledge often can only point toward truth, not lay it out cleanly. That is often the way of it, do you not think? We always want someone to tell us the answers, but often the only way important answers can be found is by our own seeking."

We were climbing a ridge now, my legs wishing we were already heading downhill again. "You know, you're really pretty smart," I admitted.

"Thank you, dearest brother!" My opinion seemed to mean a lot to Kari, who seemed bashful at what I had said.

"Are you some kind of special person?"

"What?"

"That Lady Amelia kneeled before you, and you didn't seem to think that was unusual," I pointed out.

"Oh." Kari waved one hand as if it didn't matter. "I am Spirit Daughter of White Lady, which makes me nobility among the unicorns. White Lady is...in human terms she would be called the queen, though that is not an exact comparison. The unicorns respect her and those such as I linked to her, but men and women take it very seriously in other ways. It is a little embarrassing, really."

"White Lady is the queen?" I said. "So you're actually a unicorn princess? A real unicorn princess? There are a lot of little girls back home who would kill to be able to call themselves that."

Kari gave me a worried look. "Little girls would be a danger to me in your world?"

"No. It's just a saying. It means they'd love to be able to call themselves that."

"What we call ourselves, and what others call us, does not change who we are. That is what matters, is it not? Not what we are, but who we are?" She took a final look back at the keep as we crested the ridge. "I believe that Lady Amelia's Keep might settle down, now, and stay in the same place. It is in a good place, is it not?"

"Yeah," I agreed. "It is. When I build my castle, I'll look for a view like that."

"There you are jesting again! I can tell this time."

I'll admit it. It was getting to be kind of fun bantering with Kari at times. Besides, I was still on a natural high from us surviving the mirror. Which reminded me of something else I had been meaning to ask her. "Hey, Kari. Seriously, weren't you worried about breaking that jewel on your sword hilt when you hammered that mirror with it?"

Kari glanced down at her sword. "No. This is the Sword of Fate."

"Which means what?"

"Well, it means the sword and I are tied. My fate to its fate." She used one finger to tap the blue jewel on the hilt. "The sapphire is linked to my spirit. Through it, my spirit destroyed the spell matrix in the mirror."

I waited a minute, but she had apparently finished speaking. "So why does that mean you didn't have to worry about the jewel breaking?"

Kari laughed in a way that started birds singing. "Because I have been raised by unicorns. Like them, my spirit cannot be broken, Liam!"

"Really?" I stared at her for a minute, then down at the grass we were walking through. "That must be amazing."

"How so? It is just who I am."

Yeah. Just who she was, the unicorn princess with the magic sword who didn't think she was a big deal. What would I have been like if I had been some prince and people actually knelt when they saw me? If I had an enchanted weapon and people thought I was special? I didn't have to guess too much. A kid who my mom and my best friend agreed thought the world revolved around him would've been a lot worse if he had been a unicorn prince. Or a lion prince or something that would be a bit more guy-like. I would have sucked up everything nice anyone said to me and taken any gifts they offered, just like that mirror had sucked up everything that mattered.

And yet, while I walked along feeling totally disgusted with myself, I remembered Kari calling me a "worthy man." At the moment I didn't feel like I was either worthy of anything or a man, but if somebody like Kari could say that, maybe I wasn't hopeless.

"Is something wrong?" she asked me.

"No. Yes. I guess I'd like to know that my spirit could be anything like as strong as that."

"I will show you what I can of how to be so strong in spirit," Kari promised, and I knew it was a promise even though she didn't say the word promise. So that's how it worked. "If we and our worlds survive, that is," Kari added.

We didn't talk for quite a while after that as Kari pushed our pace again. I had a lot of thinking to do and had to concentrate on breathing, and even she seemed to be feeling a bit worn by how fast we were going. After slogging through knee-high grass for a long time it was a relief when our path merged with a dirt track heading the direction we wanted to go. Then the dirt path crossed a wider dirt road which curved off to our left, heading into a large wooded area. A wooden signpost adorned with strange symbols stood at the crossroad. Kari paused a moment to examine it, while I pretended not to be grateful for the chance to stop.

Kari shook her head. "It would be quicker, perhaps, but we cannot risk that way," she declared, pointing down the larger road.

"Why not?"

"It is elven," she replied shortly, proceeding down the smaller dirt track again.

I hastened to catch up. "That's bad?"

"Chancy at best," Kari advised. "Our odds of leaving that forest alive would be very small." Our own path converged with the same woods the bigger road had entered, running just outside the trees. I stared into the shadows, feeling the afternoon sun beating down on me and wishing we were in the shade.

I realized someone was staring back.

"Keep moving," Kari hissed at me.

I discovered that I had slowed down a lot and tried to match her pace again. "I think there's somebody in those woods watching us."

Kari didn't look toward the woods, but she nodded. "Unfortunately, there is. Some of the elves have noticed us, but do not think of them as somebody. You cannot consider elves in the same light as you would humans such as us."

I gazed into the woods again, their edge not more than maybe twenty feet from us now, and finally saw pairs of eyes scattered under the trees. The eyes were bigger than a human's should be, but even though they weren't that far away I couldn't read any emotion in them. I could see only the vaguest impressions of the bodies attached to the eyes, so whatever was watching us was really well camouflaged. But what Kari had said worried me because it sounded kind of mean. "What, they're not as good as us or something?"

She gave me a baffled look. "Elves? They are different in ways which make them dangerous."

That didn't really clarify things. "So I should be worried?"

"Yes." Kari loosened her sword in its sheath with exaggerated motions, which I guess were supposed to make them obvious to the elves watching us. "And no."

"That helps. Look, could you tell me what elves are like?"

She looked at me, her face hard. "They are elves. They are *different* from humans. Not smarter or less smart, not better or worse, not wiser or less wise. They are different, and do not think and feel as we do. They are not hostile, because they do not care enough about us to consider us enemies. But that does not mean some of them might not decide to strike us."

I tore my eyes away from the woods. "Why are they watching us if they don't care about us?"

"Have you never watched an insect scuttle across the grass, Liam?" That wasn't a very comforting comparison. "Have you ever seen someone decide to step on that insect, just because they can? Or to tear the wings from a fly because they consider its suffering cause for amusement?" That was a worse one. "So it is between elven-kind and human."

"They think they're that much better than humans?" I asked, thinking that these elves didn't sound much like the ones I had read about.

"No! It is not that the elves think themselves better, but that they are so different that they regard us as we do ants." Kari tapped her sword. "But they can see I carry a sting and that should dissuade them from attacking. That and what I wear." This time she stroked one hand along the circlet she wore over her hair. "Few humans wear items woven from hair gathered from the manes of unicorns. It will tell the elves who I am, and that an attack on me will be as an attack on White Lady from the unicorns' point of view. That *may* discourage the elves."

"If they know who you are then—" My mind finally engaged and I stopped talking.

But Kari knew what I had been going to say. "That means nothing to them, Liam. If I were to meet the elven lady who birthed me she would still regard me as beneath notice." She blew out a long breath. "They are not evil, and among themselves there is love I am told, but they cannot see us as their equals, or even worthy of compassion or empathy."

I swallowed and nodded. "I've met some adults who're kind of like that. As far as they're concerned, kids don't even exist. Our opinions don't matter. Nothing about us matters."

"It is odd, is it not, how hatred can feel preferable to indifference?" Kari asked.

"Yeah, odd." I took another look at those cold eyes watching us without real interest from the shadows of the forest, remembering some old fantasies that I had read. "You know, modern fantasy in my world tends to portray elves and stuff like that as beautiful and romantic and neat. But the old stories from my world were all about elves being dangerous and cold, like they'd use humans like pets until they got bored and then they'd cast them aside."

"The old stories of your world seem to have had much truth to them. Perhaps your world once had elven-kind as well."

"Yeah. Maybe." Or maybe Kari and I weren't the first humans to have ever crossed between her world and mine.

With those eyes watching us, I forgot for a while how tired my legs were getting and just concentrated on keeping up with Kari. If her sword and her hair-circlet made her look like a hornet to the elves, then Liam the ant wanted to stick close to her. I strained my ears for any sounds the elves might be making, but all I could hear was the unending tramp of our feet, the occasional sighing of the wind through the nearby trees, and the constant background music of bird song.

Unfortunately, the landscape still rolled a bit, with small elevations and small depressions alternating as the path we were on headed across them. That meant there were times when we couldn't see very far ahead.

As we approached one of the rises, two elves suddenly appeared from the other side, moving with such speed that they just sort of popped into position right ahead of us. Kari and I came to a halt while I stared.

One of the two elves was male, I think, and the other a female, I think, though both were very tall and slim, with long, skinny legs and arms that still looked real strong. They had those big eyes and pale hair on their heads which stood up in punk spikes that seemed natural rather than some hair style. Both had on some sort of lightweight, dark upper body armor that gleamed in the sun, and both wore swords with slender blades and sharp points. They just stood there, not looking directly at us.

Kari nudged me to the right. "Do not meet their eyes. Go around them," she whispered in a very low voice.

I started going that way, Kari right beside me, but stumbled to a stop again when a third elf appeared on that side. Kari pulled my upper arm to the left and we started edging in that direction, only to have a fourth elf appear blocking us there.

"Why do I think I know what I'll see if I look behind us?" I asked Kari.

"There are two more there," she answered.

Six elves against two of us. There didn't seem any reason not to meet their eyes now, so I did.

And regretted it.

You know how on TV or in movies aliens are pretty much humans with funny ears or funny foreheads or lots of fur? They look a bit different, or a whole lot different, but inside the aliens are all basically people in the way they think and feel. It's the same for different races in fantasy, who are all people in different ways. In stories, even computers that gain intelligence act just like human beings. And you know how you can look into the eyes of, say, a cat or a dog and know they aren't thinking quite like a human, but still you can sense some common ground, some shared emotions in those animals?

The elves weren't like any of that. I looked into their eyes and saw...nothing. Nothing I could recognize. Like Kari had said, different. Combined with their long, lean arms and legs it conjured up an image of really big insects, something that really didn't think like humans at all, something that was intelligent but not in the same way we were.

But as I stared at the elves surrounding us, I thought I could recognize something, and then I realized what that something was. The elves might think and feel differently, but some of the ways they acted I could grasp. These elves felt like schoolyard bullies, projecting that same casually cruel attitude which said they didn't really care about what happened to someone or something else, that they were ready to inflict a little pain and suffering on whatever got within reach just for fun. Only unlike schoolyard bullies, who were human after all even though they didn't seem like it a lot of the time, these elves wouldn't stop at just humiliating and hurting us a little bit.

Kari, moving very slowly, grasped her sword and drew it, bringing it around in front to a guard position. She spoke in a loud, clear voice. "I am Kari, She Who was Born to Elven-kind, Bearer of the Sword of Fate, She Who Is Apart, and Spirit Daughter of White Lady of Eveness."

The elves didn't seem impressed by any of Kari's titles, still not looking directly at her, and again exchanging glances in which I probably imagined seeing malicious amusement. First one elf, then another, stepped closer to us in blurs of motion. Man, they were fast. Forget trying to run away.

"They don't care," I said out loud, knowing that I sounded baffled. "They're not messing with us because they hate us, but just because they don't care whether or not we get hurt."

"That is what I told you, dearest brother," Kari agreed, taking a deep breath and raising her sword higher so the blade caught the sun and flashed.

The threat seemed to impress the elves, as they paused in their advance, but I didn't think it would work for long, and I didn't have anything to threaten the elves with. No branches anywhere nearby, nothing but pebbles on the path. Without really thinking about it I patted my pockets as if I might have left, say, a hand grenade in one of them and forgotten about it.

What I touched wasn't a weapon. Copying Kari's slow, deliberate motions, I reached into my pocket and pulled out my phone. Still no bars or connection, of course, but the screen lit up just fine.

Now what? I couldn't call nine-one-one for help, and the elves didn't look like they would be amused by the dumb videos I had downloaded, or any of the game applications. That left... "Kari, what kind of music do elves like?"

She took her eyes off of the elves long enough to give me a look like she thought I was crazy. "I do not have my harp, Liam, and even if I did—"

"Just tell me, what kind of music do they like?"

Another elf did the blur movement forward as the circle around us contracted a little more.

Kari swallowed before she could answer, pivoting slowly to keep her sword before the closest elves. "String instruments. Harps, mandolins, liras—"

"Liras?"

"They're also called violas. Liam, what—?"

"Okay. Acoustic strings. Got it." What music did I have on my phone that featured acoustic strings? Despite my growing nervousness I tried to think. Harps, no. Violins, not sure. Guitars...

Guitars.

I tapped frantically, bringing up the hot Spanish/Rock guitar album. Setting the external speaker to max volume, I started playback and set it to repeat until the battery ran out.

The phone's external speaker wasn't any surround-sound wonder, but in the near-silence of Kari's world it provided enough volume to be heard clearly. The elves stopped moving, their heads turning slightly from side to side as if trying to find the source of the music. Kari gave me an amazed glance, then focused back on the elves, apparently trusting me to know what I was doing.

But what did I do now? It had worked to distract the elves, but that would only help if I ditched the phone. I looked down at it, hating the idea. I had really downloaded a lot of stuff and personalized it and...and, it was just a *phone*. I mean, so what? I could get another one. It might take a few months, since Mom and Dad would be real unhappy with me for losing this one and would make me sweat it out a while to teach me a lesson about taking care of my stuff and *blah, blah, blah,* but that would be a whole lot easier to endure than having these elves rip off my arms so they could watch me flop around in the dirt for a while. Worse, they would do the same thing to Kari. Sometimes you just have to set priorities, and when you get right down to it, she was my sister and my arms were kind of important to me, too, and junk really is just junk even if the junk is a smart phone.

So I extended my arm out from my side, and the eyes of the elves focused on the phone. "Yeah," I coaxed them. "Shiny! Pretty music! Lots more fun than tearing up a couple of kids, right?" I looked toward the forest, then tossed the phone in a low arc toward it, praying that the thing would land in the grass softly enough to keep working.

It did, the guitar notes still ringing out as the phone bounced to a stop.

The elves waited for a long, heart-stopping moment, then bolted in a group toward the phone almost too fast for me to see them move. Kari's hand hit my back an instant later. "Run!" she ordered.

I ran, Kari beside me, over the nearest crest and down the other side, the pounding notes of *Diablo Rojo* fading gradually as we put distance between us and the elves as fast as we could. Sorry, Rodrigo y Gabriella, but I could replace a download easier than I could any of my limbs or vital organs. We didn't stop running until the music could no longer be heard, and then we only slowed to a really fast walk.

Kari started laughing softly as she gasped for breath. "Dearest brother, how fortunate that you, too, had an enchanted object!"

"It wasn't really enchanted," I explained, wheezing and worn out. "The phone works by science."

"The Archimaede says that enchantments are just science beyond the science we know," Kari said.

"He does?" I thought about it. "I bet he's right."

"The sacrificing of your fone was a noble act," Kari continued, smiling at me.

"Ah, it wasn't any big deal. It's just a phone." A week ago I wouldn't have said that. This morning I wouldn't have said that. But I had realized while facing the elves that it was true. Just a phone. Not having it wouldn't change my life. And not having the newest, best phone as a replacement wouldn't matter all that much, either. "Yeah. Just a phone. No big deal."

Kari gave me another smile, a smile like she was proud of me again, and that felt like a big deal. Her expression turned thoughtful as she looked back the way we had come. "Your fone is an object from your world. But it, like you, is newly come to Elsewhere. It should not cause problems for some time, and since we can describe it for the Archimaede and tell him who has it he can retrieve it." She rubbed the side of her face, unhappy. "Still, it does not feel proper to leave such an object for others to deal with. If time permits, Liam, perhaps we can make an attempt to recover it."

"You want to deal with the elves again?"

"It's not what I want, it's what I ought to do," Kari explained.

"Oh. You mean like Frodo."

"Frodo? Is this Frodo a friend of yours?"

"No, he was just somebody who had to do something important."

After about what I guess was another half hour but felt a lot longer, the path we were on finally began curving away from the forest. We climbed up another long slope, my legs burning with the effort, then as we descended the other side finally losing sight of the elven woods. Kari sighed with relief at getting away from the woods while I sighed with relief at being able to walk downhill for a while.

After that the path wore along, up and down and mostly in the open. At one point, a flock of birds so numerous it covered the sky flew past, leaving us in shade for what must have been five minutes. Otherwise, the sun stayed bright and hot in a cloudless sky of the most amazing, brilliant blue, and since we had turned inland the breeze had lost its sea cool and become dry and warm. We finally came to a place where a small stream cut across the path, its bright water laughing over smooth stones.

Kari stopped and stared at the sky while I knelt down by the stream. "Is this water safe to drink?"

Kari pointed into the stream. "The fish believe so."

I saw the tiny fish shapes flitting by under the clear water and grinned. The water was cooler than I'd expected and it tasted wonderful. I drank several handfuls, washing the dust out of my throat, while Kari drank some as well and poured a few handfuls over her head. When she straightened, she shook her head, sending droplets flying. "Surely our goal cannot be much farther."

I shaded my eyes and squinted at the sun as well. "How far are we from the Archimaede's place, anyway?"

To my surprise, Kari pointed without hesitation. "That way. Following the land, we've gone over and then back, so when we return we'll be able to cut across directly and it won't be as far. But making the distance before sunset won't be an easy journey if we don't come across the well of fire soon."

I was thinking that the journey hadn't been all that easy already when my stomach made a rumbling comment of its own. "Sorry."

Kari grinned. "It is well past the noon-day meal."

"Tell me about it. I could eat a horse."

"That would not be wise, Liam. If we had a horse it would be better employed helping us travel."

"I know. It's just an expression." My stomach growled again. "You don't happen to have any trail mix on you, do you?"

"Road food?" Kari shook her head again. "No." She looked around carefully, then smiled. "I believe there is an old orchard gone wild over there, Liam. There may well be fruit."

Fruit. My stomach grumbled approval. "Let's go."

"It is a little ways off our path." Kari scanned the skies and frowned. "Just our luck that there are no birds at hand to ask whether that orchard has ripe fruit."

"I guess we'll have to walk there and find out."

"No, Liam, that is not necessary. I can tell you are not as accustomed as I am to long journeys on foot. This will be a chance for you to rest. I will check the orchard and come back."

I know it's dumb, but the idea that I had to rest while Kari could keep going stung my pride. "I'm all right."

"I did not say otherwise," Kari replied. "You have kept alongside me without complaint. But we have no idea how much farther we must go this day or what we must face when we reach the end."

It made sense. I knew it made sense. And I was the guy who had pulled Kari back from the place where all dreams are dead. It wasn't like I needed to stand on my pride over taking a break. "Okay. I'll wait here."

Kari grinned, obviously relieved. "I will be back in two sweeps of a gryphon's wings!" she promised, before leaping nimbly across the stream and set off toward the trees.

I sloshed through the stream after her, loving the feel of the cool water around my overheated feet, then sat down heavily on the grass along the far bank, wondering why the characters in fantasy books never complained about their feet throbbing with pain after trudging along for hours. But at least the throbbing in my feet kept me from noticing the aching in my legs as much. I wondered how long it took a gryphon to sweep its wings.

Meanwhile, Kari jogged off toward the orchard like she had been resting all day. I watched her, still trying to decide what I thought of her. What I thought of everything. When she had been in danger in the mirror I had just been thinking of saving her life. I hadn't really been thinking about long-term stuff. But hey, Liam Eagan, she's coming home with you when this is all done. Assuming we and the walls between worlds survived, that is. Life won't be the same. I still wasn't sure how I liked that. I was slowly coming to the conclusion that Kari was okay, for a girl, I guess, and twice now she had used that sword to save us both. But it's not every day a sister walks into your life. Especially one carrying an enchanted sword.

Just about then somebody yelled. "Hey! Liam!"

I looked in the direction of the voice and couldn't believe my eyes. I had decided that things like unicorns and castles that appear out of nowhere were just the kind of stuff you had to expect in Kari's world, but I hadn't expected to see my best friend from back home. "James?" He was standing by the side of the path, on the other side of the stream, grinning at me. "How'd you get here?"

"I walked," James said. "Just like you."

"But I was with Kari. Boy is she going to be surprised to see you."

"Kari? You're still with her?" James's grin faded and he shook his head.

"Yeah." I was sure my own voice didn't sound too happy that time. "What?"

"Nothing. Come over here so we can talk."

"Why don't you come over here?" I pointed back toward the orchard. "I'm waiting for Kari."

"Liam, she's not important. I mean, really. Some girl you just met today? Come on."

I shook my head. "When you met Kari at the school you said she was my sister."

"Did you believe me?"

"Uh...no."

James nodded. "Liam, from the moment she showed up at Hillcrest she started getting you into trouble. What kind of nut brings a sword to school? And dresses like that? Do you want everybody pointing at you and saying that's Liam, the guy with the scary sister who looks like she escaped from a game? Let's go, before she gets back and ruins everything. Before she ruins your *life*."

I have to admit that I didn't like thinking about Kari doing her clueless routine around my friends. And she might insist on wearing those same clothes. And the sword might be a little hard for people back home to adjust to. But... "James, if she doesn't come home with me, she won't have any place to go. She can't stay here."

"Who told you that?" James asked. "She did, right? Her and that weird, talking beaver."

"Yeah," I admitted, "but—Hold on, how did you know that?"

"I told you. I've been with you, man. Because I'm your friend," James insisted, "and I care about *you*. Come on, over here."

It didn't seem like a big deal to walk across the stream to him, but for some reason I didn't want to. "James, I'm waiting here for Kari."

"Why?"

I felt reluctant to tell him what Kari and I were doing. It did sound kind of off-the-wall. "Well, there's this quest, and we have to, um—"

"And you bought all that?" James sounded pitying. "Have you seen even one bit of proof for all this stuff they've been telling you? That she's your sister? That you have to save the universe?"

"Two universes," I corrected. "We did find a wristwatch at the keep, and—"

"They set you up, Liam," James insisted. "Set you up to make you go through all that pain while they filmed it for everyone to laugh at when it's posted online."

"Huh?" The strange thing was, James was bringing up everything that had been sitting in the back of my mind bothering me, all the little doubts which I had dismissed or hadn't really focused on. Was this all a reality show come-on? "How could a reality show have faked all this? The Forest of Doom and the Archimaede and—"

"Green screens," James said. "Computer graphics. Come here and I'll show you."

Something about all of that did not sound right, but I realized I was having trouble thinking. My brain felt like it was wrapped in packing foam and something was urging me to stop arguing with James because it was too hard and I should just go with him.

But, you know, along with all of my other not so great qualities I could be pretty stubborn when someone is trying to make me do something. Just ask my mom and dad. "I have to wait here for Kari," I said, the words coming out slowly.

"Why?" James demanded. "So she can make you feel bad about yourself?"

"Uh..."

"She does, doesn't she? She makes you feel like you have to change the way you do things. Is that what a friend does, Liam? Now, come here, before she gets back!"

James had that much right. Kari had made me feel a little bad about myself. I wavered, one foot taking a step closer to James. "But, she never said anything bad about me."

"Helpless? Noisy as a herd of trolls? Either of those ring a bell?"

"Oh, yeah, she did say that." What was wrong with my head? "How did you hear her?"

"I can be quiet when I want to be," James said, extending one hand toward me. "Come here."

My other foot took another step closer, while I tried to clear my thoughts. Had there been something in that water I drank? "I can't—You don't walk out on people, James. It's wrong. That's like when that guy tried to take the ring and then the orcs attacked and—"

James reached out toward me again. "Come here, Liam. Think about what happens when this is over. Everybody's going to think she's a freak. Which means they're going to think you're a freak, too. Do you think girls like Tina are going to want to hang around with you if you've got a freak for a sister?"

For some reason, that made me angry enough to think a little clearer. "Since when do you know so much about girls?"

"And old lady Meyer! You'll be toast the next time she sees you and asks where that sword is." I felt my stomach knot up at the thought of that. "You helped Kari. You're going to take the heat for her stealing it out of Meyer's office, Liam. As long as you stay with her, you're responsible for whatever crazy stuff she does. But if you're with me, you'll be fine. Life just like it's always been."

Life just like it's always been. That should have been the ultimate argument, right? I mean, that's why I originally agreed to come here, to get rid of Kari so my life wouldn't change.

But what about life just like it's always been was all that great?

I hadn't said anything else, but James shook his head. "You're already afraid of her."

"Huh?" That was about all the argument I was capable of by that point, my head felt increasingly foggy.

"Prove you're not afraid of her, Liam. Come here. Right now."

"I'm...supposed...to...wait...here." My feet were trying to move again, to get me closer to James, but I literally dug in my heels to hold them in place.

"What, like you're her dog? Wait here, Liam. Good boy, Liam," James piped in a high-pitched voice. "You don't have to do what she tells you to do."

"No. Stay...here." James's arguments had changed, I realized. It was like we were five years younger and daring each other, calling each other chicken, trying to get the other to do something stupid. Guys do that. It's how we show we like each other.

James flickered for a moment, like an image on a computer that couldn't maintain the frame rate, causing me to blink rapidly at him, and then his arguments changed, too. "You'll lose that spare bedroom, Liam. You'll lose the new TV, and you'll have to share everything with a *girl*. Including the bathroom, which she'll fill up with girl stuff. She'll take everything that's yours by rights. Just come here now, and we'll go back to the way things have always been, the way you deserve them to be. You with all your stuff for yourself."

I faltered again, and one foot took another step, but that made me really mad, because suddenly I was thinking of Kari standing there facing those wolves because she trusted me and here I couldn't even defend her against some pretty stupid and selfish arguments. My anger hit the fog filling my brain and my thoughts cleared a little. "What's the matter with you?" I demanded. "You sound just like—"

It hit me then, and I had to stand there staring at him for a moment before I could finish. "You sound just like me."

Every argument that James had made, everything he had brought up, had been lurking in my own head.

Talk about looking into a mirror and really seeing yourself.

"Hey," James said, his image flickering again in a funny way. "Why is that bad? Come here so we can talk about it."

"Without Kari?"

"Right. Come on."

James was only talking about crossing the stream, but somehow it felt like a lot more than that, like if I crossed the water I'd be leaving Kari for good. Leave Kari, who was counting on me to watch her back, like I had against the wolves, and in the keep, and when we faced off against those elves. Abandon her...like she had been by the elves. I remembered the elves and those cold, disinterested eyes empty of anything I could connect with, and when I looked at James I saw the same thing in his eyes. My brain really cleared, at that point, fear and anger working together to get my neurons firing right again. "Listen. I'm not leaving Kari. End of discussion." I thought I could hear someone yelling, off in the distance, but I couldn't turn away from watching James.

James waved his hands. "That's it. I've had it. Me or her, man. You decide. Right now."

"I already did decide. Who are you? James wouldn't act like this."

"You know who I am, Liam." He flickered a third time, then Tina was standing there instead of James, smiling at me and holding out her hands. "Hey," she said, "Come here."

"Tina?" This had gotten really weird, but my brain had become cloudy once more and couldn't figure out just what was wrong with it. And Tina was smiling at me and beckoning to me, and man did she look good.

"Come here, Liam," Tina whispered, one hand going to the buttons on her shirt. "Help me get this off."

"Uh…" I was standing right near the edge of the stream now, my resolve totally crumbling along with my ability to speak coherently. But a tiny part of my brain must have still been working, because I suddenly wondered why Tina would be acting all hot and eager toward me when she wouldn't even talk to me this morning. I don't understand much about girls, but that still didn't make any sense. Trying to understand her changed attitude, I looked into Tina's eyes…and saw the same emptiness. That brought me back to my senses. I wouldn't take another step, no matter what.

Whatever it was that looked like Tina held out her hand, reaching for me across the water still separating us. "Come here," she urged, reaching farther. I stared at her hand, noticing for the first time that it seemed a whole lot thinner than Tina's hand ought to look. Almost skeletal.

"What are you?" I said, too terrified to move. The yelling behind me was louder, but I still couldn't understand it, or take my eyes off of the image of Tina before me.

"Last chance, Liam." But her voice had become thin and weak. The hand kept reaching and kept getting thinner, the bones showing clearly now, but something seemed to be keeping it from crossing the stream between us. I looked at what I had thought was Tina, and before that James, and saw that whatever it was had gotten a lot thinner, too. Just skin stretched over bones, one arm reaching out way too far, grasping for me. Behind her, or him, or it, or whatever, a large hole loomed in the dirt.

"I don't need a last chance," I said. "I'm not stupid enough to listen to you."

The thing seemed to get pulled back into the hole in a flash, then the hole sealed up with a snap, disappearing without a trace, and I was staring around wondering why I felt so cold.

"Liam!" Kari was running full tilt toward me, her drawn sword held in one hand, looking frightened for the first time I could remember. It had been her yelling, I realized. "Brother! Are you all right?"

I stepped back from the stream, shaking my head to try to clear it. "What happened?"

Kari skidded to a halt near me, still anxious as she looked at my face, gasping with relief as she saw that I was okay. "I am so sorry, dearest brother. I saw it, but I was too far away to help you. I should have guessed that a wight might be around here. That is why there were not any birds."

My brain was getting back to normal, but it took a little bit of time for what she was saying to make sense. "A wight? That was some kind of monster?"

"Could you not tell at the end? They take on the appearance of someone you trust and try to lure you into their hole. Fortunately, that one was on the other side of the stream and could not cross running water to grab you while you were confused by its glamour."

Kari was gasping for air as she tried to catch her breath after an all-out run. She must have been totally scared for me. I stared at her, then at the place where the hole had been. "How did it know so much?"

"About what?"

"Me. You. The stuff we've been doing. It told me all sorts of things about that."

"Oh." Kari nodded, then tapped her head with one finger. "It knew nothing. It said nothing."

"Kari, I was here, you weren't, and that thing was talking to me! We argued about all kinds of stuff!"

"No! Really! Liam, the wight does not speak at all. It makes you create something in your own head that expresses what you fear or desire. It makes you see the person or creature most likely to convince you to come to the wight. You were not arguing with the wight, you see. You were arguing with *yourself*."

Of course. I had already figured that out but hadn't yet connected the dots. "James" had been bringing up everything I had been worried about, even things I hadn't admitted to myself I was worried about. I really had been my own worst enemy.

And Tina. Oh, man. It had almost nailed me there.

"Who did you see?" Kari asked.

"James. My best friend. You met him at Hillcrest." She nodded. "And, uh, I saw...this girl."

"Oh." The way that Kari said that made it sound like she knew what that vision might have involved. "Your girlfriend?"

"I don't really have a girlfriend. At the moment," I added quickly, as if I just happened to be between girlfriends right now.

Kari smiled reassuringly at me. "It is well that you are so strong, my brother."

Strong? Me? All I had done was...face up to my fears and refuse to listen to them. And use my head when my hormones just wanted to get down to business. Hey. Not bad.

But now I looked at Kari and got worried again. "You're really Kari?"

"Yes, Liam."

"But you said the wight makes itself look like someone you trust, and..." I didn't want to come out and say it, but I had to. "I think you're the person I trust the most now."

Her face lit up with understanding, but instead of saying anything Kari took a couple of steps to stand in the stream.

"And?" I asked.

"Running water, Liam. It would destroy the wight, cause it to come apart like fat in a fire."

"It would make the wight dissolve?" That would have been cool to see. Too bad the thing hadn't leaned a little too far over the water when it tried to get me. I grinned at Kari. "Thanks."

She walked out of the water and gave me another one of those affectionate shoulder punches. I was going to have one serious bruise there before the day was over. "You are most welcome." Kari glanced at where the hole had been. "A wight's hole is cold, with nothing of fire to it, so that cannot be the guardian of the second object we seek. You and I should try to dig the wight out of its hole and destroy it, but that would be too dangerous a task for just the two of us, even had we the time. I will tell the unicorns of the wight and they will see that it is dealt with." She gave me a worried look and bowed slightly toward me. "I hope that you will forgive me for leaving you alone, dearest brother. If we had only stayed together—"

I slapped my forehead. "Oh, man! I just realized. We broke the 'don't-go-off-by-yourself rule!'"

Kari stared at me. "The what rule?"

"The 'don't-go-off-by-yourself rule'," I explained. "In movies, when there's a group of people and something scary is after them, they always wander off one by one and when they're alone the scary thing nails them."

"Always?" Kari was looking baffled again. "If this always happens, why do the people go off alone?"

"Because they're, like, not thinking! Just like you and me! I don't know how many times I've watched that happen."

"Oh." Kari nodded slowly. "The rule means you should stay together for safety?" I nodded back. "That is a wise rule. How many of your friends have died because they did not heed it?"

"Uh...none. That I know of."

"But you said that you have seen—"

"Not for real." I grinned as Kari glowered at me. "Sorry. I've just seen a lot of stories that teach lessons like that." I wondered if Mom would believe me when I said those flicks had taught me something important.

"Oh. Like the lessons the Archimaede gives me?" Kari smiled again, mollified, and reached into the big pockets on the sides of her shirt and pulled out a bunch of small apples. "I found these. I hope they will do."

"They're a lot better than nothing. Thanks, again." I took several of the apples, and we started walking. I was warming up again pretty fast under the bright sun. I looked back once to where the wight had tried to get me. If I hadn't had enough sense to recognize when my own fears were getting out of hand, I'd be in that hole right now.

Still, there were a couple of things I maybe should be concerned about. "Kari?"

"Yes?"

"Do you keep a lot of stuff in the bathroom?"

She gave me a disbelieving look. "That is a very personal question!"

"It's my bathroom, too!"

"What does that have to do with it?" Kari demanded.

"I just want to know!"

"It is personal! It is private! I cannot believe that you asked that!"

"Excuse me for living," I grumbled. *Girls*.

"Boys," Kari muttered.

CHAPTER SEVEN

A WALK THROUGH THE WELL OF FIRE

KARI WAS STILL STEAMING FROM THE GREAT BATHROOM Argument when our path entered another forest, which I guess was free of elves because she didn't seem especially worried. In her anger, she was setting a pace that I feared would literally be blistering my poor feet. "Kari?"

"*What?*"

That one word scorched me almost as bad as the ordeal in the mirror, but I had kept going during that and I could keep going now. "Don't you think it's a little funny? We must have set some kind of record, a brother and sister on the first day they met arguing over a bathroom we haven't even started sharing yet. As a matter of fact, we were arguing over sharing a bathroom that isn't even in the same world as we are."

Kari frowned, then the storm clouds gradually began to lift from her face and a reluctant smile showed. "I once asked the Archimaede how I would know my brother when I met him," she said solemnly, "and the Archimaede answered that I would know he was my brother by the way in which we related to each other. I thought perhaps it was only a play on words, but now I think there was another meaning there."

I laughed. "Yeah. I do, too. I can't recall ever having a more ridiculous argument over anything." I looked over at Kari, who had slowed down a little bit. "Did you know about me? Before today I mean? Because I didn't know about you. I mean, before today I didn't know I knew about you."

Kari gave me a wistful glance. "No. White Lady and the Archimaede knew. I don't know how. But they did not tell me because they knew of no way to reunite me with you. Why torment me with knowledge of a family I could never join? But then the walls between worlds weakened. The Archimaede saw the danger, and the opportunity. With the walls weakened, I could cross them, and I could bring you back to help do what was needed to restore the walls. So you see, I only learned of you a short time before you learned of me."

"How'd you find me? How'd you know to go to Hillcrest?"

Kari shrugged. "I am not entirely sure. Again, the Archimaede understands. He said I would be drawn to you when I walked through the walls between worlds. Like to like. I walked and thought of you, which I tell you was very hard because I had no idea what you looked like, and when the trees thinned I found myself in front of the grim fortress of Hillcrest. I felt I should walk inside, which I did, and then someone called my name (alas, it was not you, but the evil Lady Meyer) and you know the rest."

That I did. What had Alice said in Wonderland? Curiouser and curiouser. Or maybe weirder and weirder. I guess those mean the same thing.

Kari bit her lip, looking nervous. "Our honored mother seemed nice."

"She is," I admitted. "I mean, for a mom."

"She...seemed discomforted when she met me."

"You might say that." I wasn't being very helpful, and I could tell that Kari was worried. "She just acted that way because she was a little nervous."

Kari's alarm faded into relief. "I see. Is Mother often nervous?"

"No. I think that only happens when Mom has a fourteen-year-old daughter appear out of nowhere."

"Elsewhere," Kari corrected. "Then it should not be a problem again, should it?" But she still looked worried.

Something finally clicked in my head. The sister I didn't have had been born to an elven lady who wanted nothing to do with her. "Mom's not like that." Kari turned her head and stared at me. "She's, well, it's been sort of a pain lately, but she really cares about me and I know she'll care about you."

"Why is that a sort of a pain for you?"

"You know." I looked at her face and it was obvious she didn't know. "I'm not a kid anymore. I want to live my own life and be a little more independent, and she wants to keep tabs on me. You know how the eyes of those elves looked? Mom's eyes will never look like that. They might be mad or happy or whatever, but they always care about me. I know that. And they'll care about you."

"Thank you, Liam." Kari smiled wanly. "I never thought to meet my real mother. How would she regard me? Would she be anything like the elven lady who wanted nothing to do with me? Would I like her? It is so important, and I know so little."

"Yeah. I guess that would be scary. But don't worry. Seriously. Mom's okay. Just don't tell her I said that." How's that for irony? I'd been the one who wanted to ditch Kari, but she'd never shown any signs of thinking I felt that way. Instead, she was worried about Mom, and if I knew Mom at all, I knew Mom would never toss out a girl like Kari even if Mom doubted she was actually her daughter. But then I hadn't been rejected at birth by someone who literally couldn't love me. "Kari, can I ask something personal? You don't have to answer."

"I think we have been speaking of personal things already, Liam. What is it?"

"There were people back at that castle. Humans. At least, they looked human. How come the Archimaede didn't take you to a human mother instead of to the unicorns?"

Kari frowned, but she answered me. "I was one apart. She Who Is Apart. That is another one of my titles, you know, but I do not like to use it."

Titles. I'd heard them, but I hadn't quite connected that. My little sister had titles. Go figure.

"She Who was Born to Elven-kind is clear enough," Kari continued. "Though I share nothing with the elves as you saw. Humans also would have treated me as an outsider. But that was not the only thing. The Archimaede believed that my arrival portended future events in which I would play a role. Being raised by the unicorns would give me skills and knowledge I could never acquire from other humans. Such as the skills to walk between worlds."

"He knew we'd be doing this someday?"

"No. That is not how it works. He sees probabilities. Different paths which the world may take. From these the Archimaede can judge what may be done to prepare. But he knows whatever he does, even simply examining the paths, will change the paths and probabilities, even if only a little, so every action must be carefully considered."

"Wow. I've heard of something like that. Heisenberg something. Yeah. Heisenberg's Uncertainty Principle." I couldn't believe that I remembered that. "The act of measuring changes what is being observed. Or something like that."

Kari smiled at me. "Then in your world you also have an Archimaede, though you call it a Heisenberg?"

"I guess Heisenberg was kind of an Archimaede." I wondered what it would have been like to have the Archimaede for a teacher. And to grow up in a world out of some fantasy. "You've been lucky."

"Have I?"

Brilliant, Liam. In exchange for those neat things she had given up the sort of life I'd had. And it had never even occurred to me what life might be like for someone like Kari, because I was comfortable and that was cool. "I'm sorry."

She forced another smile. "Oh, Liam, it is not your fault."

No, but a while ago I had been planning on ditching her so I could go back to living my happy, self-centered life. "Uh, yeah. Anyway, you don't have to worry about Mom."

"Thank you, Liam. How about Father? Is Father a good man?"

"He's, um, yeah." He tried. I knew that. I didn't know why Dad and I got mad at each other so much nowadays and got into arguments. "He's a good person, who tries really hard."

Kari let out released tension in a sigh. "Oh, that is wonderful! I will try so hard to be a good daughter to Mother and Father. I am an excellent hunter, tracker, and scout, and very good with a sword and bow, and I can weave tapestries, and play the harp, and I can sing as humans do or sing to just about any bird in their tongues, and I speak passable elvish, and can ride all manner of beasts, and read the winds and—"

I held up a hand to stop the flow of words. "And walk between worlds. Kari, I think Mom and Dad are going to like you."

"Do you? My elvish grammar is weak. I cannot grasp the irregular temporal tenses."

Irregular temporal tenses? And to think I'd been complaining about learning English grammar. "Kari, I'm absolutely positive that weak elvish grammar won't bother Mom and Dad at all."

She sighed again. "I am so relieved to hear that from you, for who knows them better than you?"

"Yeah." I did know my parents, right? I'd been living with them for...like...forever.

What exactly did Dad do in his job? What did Mom like to do when she wasn't working? Suddenly, I was really glad that Kari hadn't pushed for more details about them.

I was still worrying over how little I seemed to know about my own parents when Kari's expression changed, becoming intent. "Do you smell that?"

"What?" I inhaled slowly. "Burning. Burnt wood?"

"Yes."

"Somebody has a campfire going?"

"Not a campfire," she corrected. "These have the smell of old ashes, and in great number." Kari shaded her eyes to look ahead, then rapidly twittered at the nearest birds. They twittered back as Kari listened carefully. "They say the forest turns dead not far ahead."

"Dead?"

"I am certain they mean it is burned. Birds do not quite grasp 'fire,' you know."

"I wasn't aware of that."

"Well, they do not. And they cannot tell me how large an area is burned because none of the birds who enter that dead region come back out again."

Burned wood. Birds that go in don't come out. "The well of fire?"

Kari nodded, but she didn't seem thrilled to know we were getting close to our goal. "I am certain it must be that. But the well of fire holds a guardian, and I fear this burnt-out part of the forest can only mean one thing, Liam."

I waited, but Kari seemed to feel whatever it was didn't need to be said. "Okay. I give up. What's it mean?"

"A dragon, of course."

Of course. A well of fire, the Archimaede had said. So we would be facing a dragon. Kari's clothes didn't seem particularly fire resistant, though the leather ought to hold up okay. I wondered how denim would do. "It could be worse," I remarked.

Kari glanced at me. "How?"

"This could be the 1970's. I could be wearing polyester. That stuff melts and sticks when it burns."

"That is another one of your jests, is it not?"

"In a whistling-past-the-graveyard sort of way, yeah."

A few hours ago I would have immediately tried to talk Kari into heading back the way we had come. But even though the idea of confronting a real dragon had my stomach knotting up again, I stayed with Kari while she marched onward. Maybe I had gained a little confidence in myself. Maybe I was actually starting to trust my crazy little sister's ability to handle things. Maybe I was too tired from hiking all over Elsewhere to think straight. Or maybe I just wanted to see a real dragon.

You know what they say about being careful what you wish for.

The path through the forest got quieter and quieter as we walked. It didn't seem like much wildlife enjoyed living near dragons. Or maybe the dragon had just eaten everything, which wasn't something I really wanted to think about. Then it was like we crossed a line. On one side, the trees were scorched but living. On the other, we could see nothing but leafless, charred, dead trunks reaching up into the sky.

The trail ran out, rapidly diminishing into a narrow footpath that simply ceased. Apparently, most creatures had enough sense to not keep walking toward a dragon's lair. We reached the end point and stood there surrounded by the dead forest and a sense that danger was very near. The only things missing to complete the menacing picture were some flying monkeys and a sign saying "I'd Turn Back If I Were You."

Kari exhaled slowly, then drew her sword. "It will not be much farther ahead, brother."

"The dragon? How much is not much?"

"Much less than a league, I am certain."

Which would have helped if I had known what a league was. I knew you could find twenty thousand of them under the sea but that was about it.

Kari raised her sword and used it to point ahead and to the right. "That way seems clearer. It will be easier for you. If you go that way, I will work my way around to the left where the fallen trees are thicker. When you get within sight of the dragon's lair, stop and wait until I draw off the dragon. That will give you the opportunity to enter its lair and find the object we seek."

"Whoa." I had abruptly snapped out of whatever mood had kept me quiet up until now. "Draw off the dragon? You mean you're going to fight it?"

Kari nodded as if fighting a dragon was the most natural thing in the world for a fourteen-year-old girl. "If necessary. I will try to avoid that, but I can defend myself."

"Have you ever fought a dragon before?" I demanded.

"Yes, of course! Several times. Well, in a group that is," Kari admitted. "Not by myself."

"But you're going to take that one on. By yourself."

"Only if I have to. I can handle it, Liam."

"What if it comes after me?"

Kari bit her lip. "That might be a problem. You don't have your sword."

"I don't have any sword, Kari. Remember? I don't have any weapon of any kind. How fast are dragons?"

"Very fast. Like the wind. A very fast wind, that is."

"Then shouldn't we come up with another plan? How can you draw off a very fast dragon and keep it occupied long enough for me to search its den or lair or whatever and not get caught myself?"

"Liam, we do not have any other choice! An out-right attack on the dragon by just the two of us would be too dangerous. I know I am asking you to take a big risk here, but we need to do this and there is not much time left in the day."

I looked upward, where the dead, bare trees provided little barrier, to see that the sun had dropped far enough to mean the afternoon had to be well along. "Yeah. I guess so."

"It will be all right, Liam. Do not worry."

Yeah. Okay. Don't worry. Her with her sword fighting a dragon single-handed. Me trying to outrun a very fast dragon. Nothing else apparently alive in this part of the forest, which sort of gave a clue as to how effective either fighting or running away was when it came to dragons. What's to worry about?

Kari gave me an encouraging smile, then went slinking off in that silent way she had, her sword ready in one hand. I stood there, watching her disappear among the dead tree trunks, and wished I had a tank. One with a really big gun and really heavy armor plate.

What could I do? Kari had told me herself that I sounded like a herd of trolls when I was trying to sneak through the woods. And not just any herd of trolls. A *loud* herd of trolls. What chance did I have of sneaking up on a dragon's lair?

Dragon's Lair. There had been a really old video game called that, where you tried something, and died, and tried something else, and died, and tried something else...

But if I just stood here, Kari would be facing that thing alone.

And even Kari, who seemed to take a lot of really dangerous things in stride, hadn't thought she had much chance single-handed against a dragon.

Hi, Mom, I'm home. Where's Kari? Well, there was this dragon and it really didn't make sense for both of us to get eaten. Oh, by the way, the universe is going to end any time now because I chickened out on her.

I hadn't come this far to give up now, or to leave my little sister to deal with a dragon alone. I know it sounds strange, because Kari seemed to be generally death on two legs when it came to fighting, but she was still my little sister, so I felt like I ought to protect her.

I looked along the path that Kari had indicated for me, and began walking as carefully as I could, trying to move in a less loud-herd-of-trolls like way. I kept looking for anything that might work as a weapon, but the only branches left on the ground which weren't burned to charcoal were way too big to use as a bat or a club, and there weren't any swords or tanks lying around waiting for me to make use of them.

I barely kept from falling over when my foot slipped on a loose rock. Well, that was something. I bent down and picked up the rock, which was about the size of a softball and felt really comforting in my hand. The next whitish, rounded object that I spotted embedded in the dirt looked way too much like the top of a skull for me to want to dig it out. I finally found another rock, slightly smaller, a little way farther on and then snuck ahead with my weapons in both hands. Big bad Liam, king of the cavemen.

The wind that had been around us since we had left the castle on the sea had finally died, leaving the air in the burnt forest totally still. It didn't feel like the stillness in the castle had, though. That had been the absolute stillness of life brought to a stop. This was the absolute stillness of death. I'd never realized just how different those two things could feel.

I couldn't hear anything except the sounds of my own movement. Every crunch and crackle of my steps on the charred ground seemed to reverberate like the thunder of a motorcycle engine. I stopped once, staring around and wondering if I should go back. But then I headed forward again, figuring that if the dragon wanted me I had already given it enough noise to find me.

Without warning, I reached the edge of the dead trees. I found myself on the verge of a slope leading down into a big hollow of bare dirt large enough around to hold an athletic field. I steadied myself against one tree, staring downward. White sticks littered the bottom of the hollow, but it wasn't until I spotted the skulls among them that I realized that the sticks were bones of animals, people, and probably other things native to Kari's world. On the opposite side of the hollow, a large cave opening gaped like an irregular mouth, scattered boulders near the entrance resembling loose teeth that had fallen free.

But I didn't spend much time looking at the cave. Perhaps a third of the way around to my left I saw the dragon. It was crouching behind the edge of the hollow, its head twitching slightly as it watched something among the fallen, burnt trees on the other side. I raised myself a little, trying to spot its prey, and after a moment I caught a flash of movement and knew. Kari.

Maybe she knew the dragon was watching her. Maybe not. She must have made a lot of noise or done something else on purpose to distract the dragon from coming after me. Maybe its dragon brain figured that it should get the quiet one first and then it wouldn't have trouble finding noisy me. I could see the dragon gathering its feet under itself, rolling its high, bony shoulders like a cat getting ready to pounce.

Now, if I had run into this in a game I would have paused it and done a save game and thought a long time about how to handle it. But here was a real dragon preparing to pounce at any moment. On my sister. No time to ponder alternatives. Never mind Kari's plan. I wasn't going to let her face that thing alone while I hid in a cave.

It's not that I didn't still think Kari was sort of nuts. But it seems that sometimes there's a fine line between being nuts and doing the right thing. I hoped I was on the right side of that line.

I tossed my first rock lightly up to judge its weight again, then pitched it as hard as I could at the monster. I switched my other rock to my good hand and did the same thing. Then I yelled as loud as I could. "Kari! Look out!"

I watched my first rock ricochet off the side of the dragon, and the second one hit near its forearm. It swung its head around at my shout, apparently not hurt in the least by my rocks, and glared at me. Instead of leaping after Kari, it twisted its whole body in one sinuous movement and launched itself toward me.

Right about then I realized that I had no idea what to do next. Maybe a little planning wouldn't have been a bad thing.

I assume you've never seen a real dragon. I hadn't. I'd always thought dragons were kind of cool, because dragons were a lot like dinosaurs and everybody knows dinosaurs are cool. It's always fun to watch dragons (or dinosaurs) romping around a movie screen or a computer screen, chomping down on anything that moved and generally tearing up the landscape.

At least, it's fun when you're not one of the guys in danger of being chomped on.

What's a real dragon look like? Don't think cool. Don't think dinosaur. Think snake. Big, big snake. With legs and wings. And eyes that have that reptile slit and look at you as just one more appetizer before it goes off to eat a bunch of cows or something.

This one was coming for me now, moving really fast. Kari's comment about dragons being as fast as the wind seemed way too accurate.

It finally occurred to me that I ought to run. But I had taken too long to figure that out. Fortunately, I slipped on the edge of the hollow as I frantically turned to run, and instead went down flat, just in time to escape a claw the size of a bowie knife slashing through the air where I had been.

This is where you came in. I told you we'd get back here eventually. Like I said, I kept sliding and rolling down the slope, right underneath the dragon, and finally pitched up at the bottom of the hollow, dazed and battered, the empty sockets of a bear's skull staring blankly back at me. Before I could even think about getting up, the dragon had jumped and landed right in front of me. The earth was still shaking from the impact when the dragon hissed at me, reared back a little and spread its jaws.

If you've never found yourself lying on the ground with a dragon opening its mouth wide as it prepares to bite off about half of your body, I don't recommend it. The teeth looked like rows of big knives, and saliva was falling onto the ground next to me and raising little columns of smoke where it landed. If I hadn't been terrified I would have spent a moment admiring the whole alien-vibe of the scene. But unlike a movie alien, this monster made it all too obvious where the term dragon breath had come from. I thought I was going to choke on the stench.

No way out, Liam. No saved game. I lay there and stared at certain death.

The jaws paused for a moment, preparing to clash shut on me. I heard a wild yell, then a sound like a hammer beating on a truck. The jaws jerked away, and that broke my paralysis. I realized I could move again. I backpedaled a few feet on the ground, trying to get some distance between me and the dragon, and I saw Kari. She was still yelling, and holding the hilt of her sword with both hands as she rained furious blows on the dragon's head. I gradually was able to understand, between the clangs of sword blows falling on dragon armor, some of what Kari was screaming at the dragon: "Leave!" (clang!) "My!" (clang!) "Brother!" (clang!) "Alone!"

The dragon darted its head this way and that, trying to escape Kari, but she bored in, slamming at the dragon's head and chipping away armored scales until the dragon leaped backward out of her reach long enough to get its balance. It hissed a cloud of noxious breath at Kari, who stood with a very grim face, holding her sword before her with both hands clasped on the hilt.

"Run!" I yelled.

"It will be upon me if I turn!" she shouted back. "We must now defeat it or die!" Kari looked awesome as she stood there, her sword's point canted toward the dragon, sweat running down her face, breathing heavily.

I stood there, feeling helpless, as the monster leaped at Kari, striking with the speed of a venomous snake. But, with perfect timing, Kari slammed her sword against the dragon's head, diverting its strike.

Before she could attack again, it struck at her once more. Then again and again, the dragon's head moving so fast on its long neck that it seemed like a hydra with eight heads. Its body hardly moved at all, forming a stable base for the monster's attacks. Kari parried every strike, but I could see the sweat coming off her and knew she must be tiring.

If I'd had a sword, too, I could have attacked the dragon while it kept striking at Kari. But as long as I was wishing for things I didn't have, why not wish for an anti-tank weapon?

I looked down, frantically searching for a weapon, any weapon. I grabbed a substantial-looking bone, but it had deteriorated so much that it cracked into fragments under my fingers.

A sword hilt was partially buried off to one side, but when I pulled on it all that was left of the sword was a thin scrap of rusted metal.

Then I saw a rusty curve of metal and yanked it out of the dirt. A shield. No decoration or anything, just a circle of metal, and not a big one. More like one of those things they call bucklers in plays by that Shakespeare guy. Round and maybe two or three times as big as a Frisbee. It had been out here a while, after whoever had once carried it got turned into dragon chow, but it still felt pleasantly hefty.

Kari barely parried the dragon's latest strike as I raised the shield. Toss it to her? I raised the shield, my hand on one edge, and realized it was a lot like a really heavy Frisbee.

No way I could hit the dragon's head, which still almost blurred as it moved. So I brought my arm back, took careful aim, and slung the shield forward in my best championship Frisbee throw, aiming at the base of the dragon's neck.

The effort of throwing the heavy shield made me pitch forward to my knees, but I kept my eyes on the disc of metal as it spun in a smooth arc straight into the dragon. It hit with a very satisfying *thunk* just above where the neck joined the body, staggering the dragon to one side. The head wavered slowly, the eyes looking unfocused, and in that moment when the dragon was dazed Kari screamed something and lunged forward, holding her sword like a spear. Driven by Kari's full weight and the momentum of her charge, the point of the sword went deep into the center of the dragon's chest.

The monster hissed like it was about to explode, rearing and tossing Kari off to the side, then fell sideways to the ground. I ran to her as the dragon flailed about, its neck coiling and writhing, scattering and splintering the bones littering the ground.

Kari had already scrambled to her feet when I reached her, but she stayed in a crouch, breathing as heavily as if she had just run a five-hundred-meter dash, her eyes fixed on the dragon. She had somehow kept her grip on the sword when she was thrown by the dragon's convulsion, but her hand holding the sword shook and she couldn't seem to raise the point from the ground.

"Can we run now?" I asked.

She managed to stop gasping for breath long enough to shake her head. "There is no need. The dragon is in its death throes."

I stood and stared again, seeing that the struggles of the monster were growing less wild as it lost strength, blood pouring out from the wound in its chest. "You killed it?"

"With your help." Kari turned a labored grin my way. "I have never seen a shield used as a weapon that way. You must show me this trick."

"Sure thing, but all I did was distract the dragon."

"That was what I needed, Liam. And you found the means to stun the creature long enough for me to deal it the death blow." She straightened up as if the effort were painful. "I could not have done it without you."

"Well...thanks. I couldn't have done it at all. Are you all right?"

She smiled again. "I am weary and will bear many a bruise from this fight." She flexed her sword arm experimentally, then took a cautious swing with the blade. "However, I have taken no serious harm. You are well?"

I checked. All my arms, legs, fingers, and toes seemed to be present. "Yeah. I think so. Thanks to you." Relief at still being alive made me blurt out something I might never have said otherwise. "You are some kind of awesome, dragon-slaying Amazon."

Kari actually looked embarrassed, sort of like a typical girl, if a typical girl happened to be holding a sword smeared with the blood of a dragon she had just killed. "I...I thank you, my brother. You call fighters in your world Amazon?"

"The ones who fight really well, yeah. Women, that is. Amazons are female fighters, you know."

"I did not know." Kari knelt to scrub her blade clean using handfuls of dirt. "Dragon blood would eat away the metal in time if not removed," she told me. "The dragon's struggles will continue for some time, but it is already dead."

"Really?" It hadn't actually sunk in until then. I had pretend-killed plenty of things in games, but had never played a part in killing anything real, let alone something like a dragon. "Dragons aren't an endangered species, are they?"

"A what?" Kari squinted at me in puzzlement. "Are you asking if dragons are dangerous? Surely you already saw the answer to that."

"No, I mean, are they, like, dying out?"

Kari's puzzlement increased. "Dragons breed rapidly. They kill each other when no other prey is to be found, but even so their numbers would grow to consume the world if not kept in check."

That was a relief. "So, killing it was a good thing."

"Of course it was." Kari shook her head at me. "Look around you. This dead land we see is what happens when dragons are not stopped. They kill everything. Now, we must waste no more time. Let us go into the beast's cave and search through its plunder. Somewhere in there must be the final object we seek."

"Uh..." I wasn't really thrilled at the idea of pawing through stuff that dragon had been squatting on for years, and my legs were still feeling more than a little unsteady from my somersaults down the mountain and the aftereffects of almost being eaten alive. But we had gone through all of that to get access to the dragon's hoard, so I just nodded. "Okay."

Fortunately, even though the cave stank of dragon, it didn't stink too badly, so apparently dragons didn't use their caves as litter boxes. I had to wait a few moments for my eyes to adjust to the dimness inside, but the cave wasn't too deep, so even its back got a little illumination from light filtering in from the entrance. Kari and I walked forward cautiously toward mounds of stuff on the floor of the cave, which slowly became identifiable as our eyes adapted to the gloom.

Lots of treasure. Lots and lots of treasure. Jewels and coins. Paintings slowly moldering away. Swords. Some of them looked almost as cool as Kari's Sword of Fate. "Can I take one of these?"

Kari eyed the blades warily. "The weapons may well be enchanted. Dragons favor such arms."

"That's not a good thing?"

"Not if you do not know what the enchantment is." She toed one of the weapons, a long sword with what looked like a big ruby set into the blade near the hilt. "These could well be accursed, like the mirror in the keep."

"Oh." I instantly lost interest in the shiny swords. "I don't think any of the swords are from my world, anyway."

We dug through the mess, Kari offering up an occasional cup or bracelet for my inspection, but all of them looked to me like they belonged here. "I have no idea what we're looking for," I grumbled. "With my luck the object is a penny or some other coin and we'll have to go through the dragon's hoard coin by coin to find it."

Kari tossed aside a gleaming gold piece. "That is certainly elven coin. Are the coins from your world gold or silver?"

"Um, neither, usually."

She frowned at me. "What are your coins made of?"

"Mostly zinc nowadays, I think, though pennies are still copper."

"Zinc." Kari shook her head. "I do not think a dragon would bother with coins of zinc. What is your most valuable currency made from?" she asked sarcastically. "Iron?"

"No. Paper."

"I was joking," she said.

"I'm not."

Kari sat back in despair. "What then would a dragon desire from your world?"

"I don't know. Video games? Auto parts? A skateboard? Soy cheese?" I made a baffled gesture. "Though none of those things could be described as not being of any world. Well, maybe soy cheese could fit that description."

"What kind of animal is a soy?"

I was trying to figure out how to explain that when my fingers ran across something with a straight edge where I couldn't really see anything. "There's something here." I concentrated on that spot, sweeping carefully, and Kari knelt nearby to feel around in the mess as well. "There. Hold on. Yeah. It's sort of cube-shaped."

I held up the object, squinting in the gloom of the cave. "It's mostly transparent."

Kari touched one side, frowning. "It is not glass, though it seems like glass."

It hit me then. "You're right. It's not glass. It's Plexiglas. There's something inside it." I held the block of Plexiglas up close to my eyes. "A rock. It's a block of Plexiglas with a rock inside it."

Kari had her own eyes up close to the other side of the block. "It does not look like a special rock. Can this be what you seek?"

"I don't know. Plexiglas is definitely of my world." I turned the thing over, checking each side, and finally found some words engraved in the Plexiglas. I squinted in the low light, trying to read, and finally made out the biggest words. "Apollo. Apollo Twelve. Wow."

"What does Apollo Twelve mean?" Kari asked.

"It means this is a moon rock. A rock from the moon."

Her eyes widened in wonder. "From the moon. Truly?"

"Yeah. The Apollo space missions went there and brought back some rocks." I grinned and held up the block of Plexiglas. "A moon rock. From my world, but not of any world. This is it."

We left the cave, blinking against the brightness of daylight. Kari took the Plexiglas cube, staring at the rock within it. "How often do the people in your world visit the moon?"

"Uh...to tell you the truth, nobody's been there for a while."

Her stare shifted from the rock to me. "You could go to the moon, and you stopped? But why?"

"I don't really know," I admitted.

"To have such a wonder, and to give it up." Kari shook her head. "I do not understand."

At the moment, neither did I. "Maybe it's like when we talked about mer-people and you sort of said, they're just fish people. Like, no big deal. Maybe people don't appreciate the wonders that are right in front of them."

Kari thought, then nodded, and gave me back the moon rock. "That may be so." She looked up at the sun. "But if we are to save the wonders of both of our worlds, we must hasten back to the Archimaede."

"I thought we'd already been hastening."

She gave me another one of those encouraging smiles. "I shall pace you. Are you ready?"

"You know the way?"

"The sun shows me the way. Onward!" She started off at a jog and I hurried to catch up, my sore feet throbbing as we went up the slope. Behind us, the dead dragon still twitched feebly as we entered the trees. "I will take us past the place where your fone was sacrificed to save us. Perhaps the elves will have tired of it and left it."

Kari kept us jogging for a while, then slowed to a fast walk, then started jogging again. As the dead trees slowly gave way to scorched trees and then living trees I managed to keep up with her. Barely.

As we slowed to a walk a second time, Kari gave me a look. "Why do you not have any girlfriends, Liam?"

I cleared my throat and spoke as carefully as I could while gasping for breath. "I've got some girls who are friends. Sort of. I guess. But I don't have a girlfriend. Right now, that is."

Kari nodded. "You are still evaluating their suitability?"

"Not exactly..."

"I can help," Kari offered. "I can see how good they are at hunting, and at use of sword and bow, and—"

"I'm not sure any of the girls I know use swords," I said.

Kari stared at me. "You said that once, did you not? That people in your world do not use swords? But when two people get together they must know that their partner is able and willing to guard their back and stand by their side against any peril."

"That's true. I hadn't really thought about it that way, but you're right." I shrugged, my breathing getting a little easier as we walked instead of jogging. "I guess in my world real partners do that without swords. You know, they still stand by each other and everything."

"I shall have to learn," Kari sighed. "Do girls in your world play music?"

"Oh, yeah. A lot of them are in bands, and lots of them sing."

"Wonderful! What else do they do?"

What did girls do? "They go shopping."

"Shopping?" Kari nodded, her face intent with thought. "You have market fairs, then?"

"Oh, yeah. Permanent ones. Big ones. Lots of clothes and jewelry and stuff. We call them malls."

She looked skeptical. "To maul something is to inflict serious damage."

"It's spelled differently. Malls in my world only inflict serious damage on credit cards."

"You will have to show me this." Kari bit her lip. "What else?"

"Um, well, sports. Soccer, track. Tina plays lacrosse. She's really good at it."

"La-cross?"

"Yeah, it's this sport where they use big sticks to fight over the ball and try to get it into the opposing team's goal."

"Big sticks?" Kari asked. "How big?"

"About this big around and maybe this long."

"And they fight another group? A team?" Kari smiled. "I think I would enjoy that."

"You'd probably be really good at it, too," I said. "I think you'd be good at any sport. Kari, it may take a little while for you to fit in, but I'm sure you'll do fine. I mean, there are no dragons to slay, but there's other stuff you can do."

Her expression brightened. "Like overthrowing the evil Lady Meyer!"

"We're going to need to talk about that." Yeah. Having Kari in my world would create some problems. But how many little sisters could whack a dragon?

Maybe being known as "Liam, brother of Kari" wasn't such a bad deal after all. Maybe it wouldn't even be a bad deal in my own world.

Kari waved forward and started jogging again, so we fell silent as I concentrated on breathing, running, and not collapsing.

The universe hadn't been saved yet.

Chapter Eight

Between the Wall of Worlds to Home

Even though my lower body was one big ache by now I managed to keep up as Kari led the way across open fields. Despite a few close calls, I miraculously didn't turn an ankle as we alternately ran and fast-walked over hill and dale, nervously watching the sun sinking toward the horizon. It would be totally harsh if we defeated both guardians and got both objects and then didn't make it back to the Archimaede before something very bad happened.

We went past the elven forest, searching the ground as we ran, but my phone was nowhere in sight. I thought maybe I heard some faint guitar notes far off in the forest, but there was no way I wanted to go in there even if we'd had time. And we definitely didn't have time.

Maybe that worry helped both of us keep going. I could finally see some signs that Kari was starting to get seriously tired, too, but we still made pretty fast time back to the river even though it seemed to take forever. The world is awfully big when you can't cruise across it at sixty-five or seventy miles per hour.

The Archimaede was standing near his beaver house when we saw him again, nervously chewing on another stick. He took it out of his mouth and waved it in greeting as Kari barreled down the river bank and gave him a hug. "Your quest is successfully completed, Kari and Liam brother of Kari?"

"Yeah." I held out the watch and the Plexiglas-encased rock. "What do we do with them? Carry them back ourselves?" Could I keep the moon rock if we did? That would be seriously cool. How many guys had a moon rock?

But the Archimaede shook its head and reached for the objects. "I must send them back. If Kari and these two objects were together as you returned home, the combined strength of their wave functions might tear a hole through the weakened walls, a hole beyond any means to repair."

"That would be a bad thing," I agreed. "But there's a third, uh, object now. My phone. We left it back near those woods'."

The Archimaede listened carefully as we described our encounter with the elves, then nodded. "It is unfortunate that you were forced to leave another object behind, but given the need I can't fault your actions. Don't worry. Kari was right. The fone is newly arrived here, so its effect on the walls is still weak. The walls will heal to almost their full strength, and then I will inform White Lady of this fone of yours, and she will demand the return of the object. Even the elven court would not defy a command of that nature from the unicorns. Once I have it, I will send it back to your world."

"I'll get my phone back?" That I hadn't expected.

"Unlikely," the Archimaede replied. "I can send it back to your world, but I have no idea where in your world it will appear."

So much for that. "Maybe it'll show up on the top of Mount Everest or something like that, and somebody will find it and it will be one of those "Believe It or Not" things."

"I cannot make any promises, Liam, brother of Kari," the Archimaede said with a grin.

"Yeah, you have to be careful about making promises," I agreed. The Archimaede reached for the watch and the moon rock, and I passed them over. As he took them, I felt the Archimaede's fur for the first time, as well as the strength in his hands. Very soft and very strong. I could see why Kari liked being hugged by the Archimaede so much.

"The returning has to be done properly," the Archimaede continued, "and it will have to be done soon. Very soon. I cannot wait until you are home, Kari, because by then the damage would irreversible. I must return them as quickly as possible, which means the walls will be healing as you try to reach home."

He gave Kari's head a pat with one giant beaver paw. "You must return to your true home quickly, Spirit Daughter of White Lady."

Kari sat back, blinking away tears as she looked at the Archimaede. "What will I do without your wisdom, Archimaede? How shall I learn all that I must know?"

The Archimaede chuckled. "Dearest Kari, wherever you find things to learn, there will you feel my presence. I have given you the tools to learn, and from that you can carry on without me. I shall miss you, but when you spark with the wonder of a new thing learned, I shall feel your joy even across the walls between worlds and know all is well."

For a giant beaver, the Archimaede sure had a nice way with words. He gave Kari a long hug, then looked straight at me.

"As for you, Liam, brother of Kari, I am pleased."

"Thanks." You wouldn't think I would care about a giant beaver's opinion of me, but I realized I did. I wanted him to think I had done a good job, and it felt good to know he did felt way. "Thank you, Archimaede."

"You've kept two of the three promises."

"I have?"

"You vowed to grasp things of great value and hold fast to them no matter the cost to yourself. You literally held on to Kari in the realm of the mirror. Held on through great pain, I might add. That's one. You also promised White Lady of Eveness that you would do whatever you could to help Kari, whether you had a sword or not. Facing down a dragon with two rocks in your hands surely fulfills that vow."

I'd forgotten that. Maybe White Lady would be a little nicer to me now. "Then there's only one promise left. I don't suppose you'd give me a hint now as to what the last promise is?"

"No. I cannot be certain what it is and cannot risk leading you astray. The last steps may be the hardest. Things are often like that. Don't worry. You've confronted the challenges and overcome them. You've confronted your fears and overcome *them*."

I stared at him. "How did you know about that? The fears thing?"

"I saw those fears, Liam, brother of Kari, before you left. You could not have succeeded had you not overcome them." The Archimaede chewed his stick a few times. "There are few certainties in the worlds, and many chances. But I knew enough to believe you would be able to deal with anything you encountered."

He canted an affectionate look at Kari. "Faith is a very powerful force. Faith in other people and powers, and faith in yourself. Kari has great faith in you."

Kari doesn't know me very well, I wanted to say. If she knew every time I'd thought about running out on her...

But the Archimaede shook his head. "What matters is what you *do*, Liam, brother of Kari. Have you not learned that yet?"

"Do you read minds?"

"No. I just understand people, even people not of this world. No one of any intelligence can encounter danger without having fears and second-thoughts. The measure of a person is how they respond to those thoughts and fears. Do they let the fears master them, do they take actions that harm others or let others come to harm? Or do they risk themselves for the benefit of others? And when they encounter something new, do they accept it without thinking, or do they question that thing and themselves in order to fully judge and understand it? You know which choices you made, and I think you made them in full knowledge of the alternatives, which is a very worthy thing indeed. You will carry the knowledge of what you can be with you from now on." The Archimaede inclined his head toward me.

Something suddenly occurred to me. "You did teach me something."

"Yes, I did," the Archimaede admitted. "Force of habit, perhaps." He turned and gave Kari a last, quick hug. "Go, now. Both of you. Kari, you know the way to your brother's home, which will now be your own, but the way will very soon be changing and not for the better. Make haste." As Kari and I scrambled up the river bank and headed back along the meadow toward the forest, the Archimaede called after us. "Liam, brother of Kari, I trust you with her! Take care of this girl!"

"That would be another promise, wouldn't it?" I yelled back.

"Yes!"

"I'll make it anyway. I'll take care of her." We had defeated the mirror and survived the elves and the wight, we had killed the dragon and made it back here. A second walk through the Forest of Doom shouldn't be all that bad.

We were jogging again, my fatigue so overwhelming now that I was mainly concentrating on not throwing up.

The unicorns were waiting for us about where we had left them, among the trees just outside the far side of the meadow. The sun had swung so low in the sky that its almost level rays were shooting in among the trees and illuminating the white unicorns so brightly that they glowed like stars in the fringes of the forest. The unicorns watched us come up, then all of them except White Lady bowed their heads toward us. I don't mind admitting it took my breath away for a moment. Well, it would have taken my breath away if I hadn't been bent over struggling to suck in air and not pass out.

White Lady came forward and caressed Kari with her muzzle. "I brought these for you." One hoof lightly touched a leather bag and a leather pack lying on the grass. "Your minstrel's harp and some of your things. But the Archimaede tells me you cannot take them, that these objects would create problems in your world just as the objects you have found created problems here. I promise you that your things will be well-looked after in case a means should ever be found for you to be reunited with them."

Kari made a sad face. "I will make a new harp in my new home, and think of you and the others whenever I play it."

"What about the sword?" I asked. The last thing I wanted was for Kari to be separated from that, but if it would cause major problems someone had to think about that.

White Lady eyed me without the suspicion she had held earlier. "The Sword of Fate is part of Kari. Your world will not see it as an object apart from her. Her headband, made from the hairs of unicorns, is also safe, for unicorns are at home in all worlds. However, her other clothing will cause problems over time."

"I must leave all my clothes here?" Kari asked. She groaned. "If I must. Is there no end to the trials of this day? Brother, please hold the Sword of Fate while I remove my clothes. I trust you not to look upon me."

"What? How can I follow you and not look upon you?" I shook my head, fending off the offered sword. "No way. That would be wrong and sick and let's not go there. Kari should keep her clothes on."

"I do not wish to do it, but if the safety of our worlds is at stake—"

To my surprise and relief White Lady shook her head at Kari. "Liam is right. The journey will be difficult enough. Attempting it without boots and other clothing would be too perilous. Trust me that the matter of your clothes can be dealt with. Now you must go. The walls between the worlds grow strong again, and if you wait too long you will not be able to get home."

"But my home is here!" Kari cried. "I have known I must leave, but now that the moment is here I cannot!"

"Hush, child. You can do almost anything you bend your will toward. Is that not so, Liam, brother of Kari?"

I hadn't expected that question, but the answer wasn't too hard. "Yes."

White Lady nodded to Kari. "Your home is with your brother, your father, and your true mother. You know this as well as I."

Kari blinked back tears. "I can never come back and visit with you?"

"You must not. The journey will be far more difficult and far more perilous for even you. You would not survive. No, you must stay in your own world. That is where you belong."

Kari let her hands drop and just stood there. "Then I will never see you again, and that hurts more than any injury ever done to me."

White Lady actually laughed, and it sounded a lot more like a human laugh than it did a horse laugh. "I am not like you, Spirit Daughter. You cannot come here, but even when the walls are at their strongest, they cannot stop me."

"I do not understand," Kari said. "I thought you could not go to my world."

"Not when it held nothing I knew. Even when the walls were weakened I could not reach your world without anything to guide me there. But once you are in that world I will be able to find it and you. Though the journey will not be simple or easy, to the guardians of the walls between worlds my presence will be like a soft breeze which passes without alarm. I can bring your clothing from this world back here when I come to see you, if," the unicorn rolled one of her eyes at me, "I am welcome."

Kari gasped with joy. "Of course you would be welcome! Would she not, Liam?"

"Ohhhhh...yeah. Mom has guests stopping by all the time. What's one more unicorn?"

White Lady gave me one of her looks. Now I was certain that she knew exactly what I was thinking. But the unicorn didn't seem to dislike me anymore. Instead, she came close enough to lightly rap the side of my head with her horn in a playful way. It still hurt, of course, and almost knocked me over. I started to understand where Kari got her punch-in-the-shoulder show of affection. White Lady winked at me. "I know now that you will take care of my spirit daughter, Liam, brother of Kari. Your spirit has grown and you no longer need conceal feelings, you even then knew, in your heart to be unworthy."

I wondered just how pale I went at that moment. "You did know what I was really thinking when we first talked."

"Yes. But we need speak of that no more. Kari believed her brother must surely have the strength to stand with her no matter the test. I accepted her belief, and you have proven her right. Rest assured that she shall return every good deed done her three-fold or more, for that is her nature. My blessing is with you until we meet again." White Lady back-stepped a few paces and tossed her head. The sun sank beneath the tree tops on the other side of the meadow and dusk fell with startling speed. "Now, go! Quickly! The day ends and the walls strengthen!"

Kari waved frantically to the other unicorns, blew White Lady a kiss, then turned and started running into the gloom of the darkening forest. I followed, staggering back into motion, trying not to run into any trees and somehow keeping up until Kari slowed her pace.

It didn't take long to figure out what Kari's friends had been worried about. This time the Forest of Doom felt a lot worse than the first trip. The forest rapidly grew wilder as we jogged along. A heavy wind started to blow among the massive tree trunks, moaning through the branches and tossing leaves and twigs down on us. The trees made menacing noises as their branches swung overhead. This time it felt like the trees weren't just guards watching us. Now they were guards out to stop us if they could. Something was still holding them back a bit, though, as if they couldn't quite get us until the walls between worlds got strong enough again. I found myself wondering how much time we had left.

The vague shadows in the gloom felt closer, too, taking advantage of the twilight to swirl in nearer toward us and still not be seen clearly. There weren't any birds. Kari glanced back at me several times, her face betraying concern. At one point she paused, looking slowly from side to side as if searching for something.

I waited without saying anything, knowing I shouldn't distract her. Finally, Kari pointed slightly off to the right. "That way." I noticed she had the other hand over her shoulder, gripping the hilt of her sword so tightly her knuckles were white, though she hadn't drawn the weapon.

I realized that I had gotten used to seeing Kari calm and confident. Seeing her worried really rattled me. "It's a lot worse this time, isn't it?"

Kari gave me that very serious look. "Yes. It is harder and harder. The walls are healing and strengthening. They are fighting our progress."

"But we can make it, right?"

"I...I think so. Liam, I did not want to worry you, but I am certain now there is also a basilisk on our trail. It is hunting us."

I had an immediate urge to spin around and look for it, but managed to stop myself. Basilisks turn anything that looks at them into stone, so just how smart would it be to look behind us to see if there was a basilisk there? "Okay. Well, if it gets too close we'll...do something."

Kari swallowed. "I cannot defeat a basilisk, Liam."

Somehow, a cheery pep talk didn't feel like the right thing at the moment, and I didn't know any specific tips for defeating basilisks. So I just nodded, made a fist, and tapped her shoulder with it. "You're not alone, Kari. We can do anything together. Look on the bright side. At least we don't have to worry about dragons."

Kari gave a snort of disbelief. "You jest even now? You are impossible."

"Look who's talking."

"Liam, I fear we cannot make it. I am so tired and the way is long and the basilisk will slowly overtake us—"

She was tired and scared. Of course she was, after a day of taking the lead while we walked between worlds and fought all kinds of things. "Kari." I waved around us. "We're walking between worlds. Today I've fought dragons and monsters and mirrors and talked to unicorns and giant beavers and right now I'm being hunted by a basilisk. Today I found out I've had a sister for fourteen years even though I've been an only child the entire time. And you're trying to tell me we can't do this?"

"Yes," she admitted reluctantly. "Though I must confess you have a point."

"Let's keep going, Kari. It can't be too much further to home, can it?"

She looked grim. "I wish I knew for certain."

"Hey, I can't lead the way, but I've got your back." That wasn't enough, I could tell. I gritted my teeth and said the two words I had hoped I would never have to say. "Dearest sister."

Kari actually smiled a bit when I said that, nodded with a look of renewed determination, and led us onward.

We kept going and things kept getting worse. The wind howled now, whipping leaves into the air to strike our clothes and faces. Large branches crashed down occasionally, some close enough to make us jump. The gloom had deepened, as if full night had come on, but it must have been a completely overcast night because there wasn't a trace of starlight or moonlight to give us any comfort. Aside from Kari, who I stayed as close to as I could without treading on her heels, all I could see in the storm-driven darkness were the dim shapes of the huge trees on all sides of us. Occasionally one of the vague, monstrous shapes would loom real close, but then veer off just before it got within reach of Kari's sword. Whenever the screams of the wind diminished for a moment we could hear the basilisk snuffling along behind us, its sounds getting closer every time. We bent over, fighting against the wind and trying to keep the basilisk on our track from seeing us.

I thought I had been scared the first time we came through this forest. I thought I had been scared when the wolf pack attacked Kari and me. I thought the mirror and everything in that castle had scared me worse than anything could. Same for the encounter with the elves, and when that dragon had been this far from biting my head off.

But I realized now that those things hadn't been that bad. Not compared to this. The funny thing was that, even though I was scared crazy, I was also able to keep going and keep my head on straight. If we had run into this on my first trip through with Kari, I would have run screaming into those dark woods or curled up into a ball and waited for something to kill me. It was that bad, the sort of fear that makes you crazy and steals every bit of your strength. But this time it didn't. I wasn't having fun, I was shaking and I felt like throwing up, but I could handle it.

Which was lucky for me, because it went on like that for a long time. I couldn't tell how far we had gone or how far we had left to go. I could only hope that Kari knew, but there was no way I was going to distract her by asking questions, even if I hadn't been worried about the basilisk hearing us talking. All I knew for sure was that the weather kept getting worse, the wind battering us and hurling leaves at our faces as if the storm was actually fighting us.

Kari finally came to a stop beside a large tree, then stood up straight, her back against it. She raised one hand and reached back, drawing her sword. Holding the sword in a ready position, she looked at me with an oddly calm expression. "You are almost there," she shouted over the wind, "but the basilisk is too close, Liam, and the walls between worlds are tightening around us. You must go before they seal. I will hold the basilisk at bay for you. Run. Now."

As much as I wanted to Run Now, something about that plan didn't make sense to me. "I can't go between worlds without you!"

"You can for this short distance when I have already opened the way. Just go, quickly!"

"You said you couldn't beat a basilisk!"

"I cannot! But I can keep it busy while you reach home!"

"What? But then you'd—" Die. For certain.

I looked in the direction of home and safety, I listened to the basilisk thumping and hissing much too close for comfort, I felt the fear in my guts that made me want to howl like a dog. And I looked at Kari, holding a sword she knew couldn't help this time, standing there desperately determined to save me no matter what it cost her. The sister who had come charging in to save me from a dragon. And now was volunteering to stay here to fight a hopeless battle while I ran for safety. This is what you wanted, right, Liam? A way to ditch this sister you didn't have, and keep everything at home centered around you?

Maybe I had wanted that, this morning. But not anymore. This morning had been a really long time ago. All of my thoughts took maybe a second this time, because I didn't even have to think about what to do. I knew the answer right away. "No!" I yelled, not caring whether the basilisk heard. "No, no, no! I'm not going anywhere without you!"

"Liam—"

"It's not going to happen! Okay, I'm scared. I'm scared out of my mind. But I promised the Archimaede that I'd take care of you. I didn't leave you in that mirror and you didn't leave me to that dragon and nobody's leaving anybody to some ugly basilisk. I'm not some stinking elf. We're a team. We're going home together or I'm staying here to fight beside you."

I'd seen Kari smile before, but not like this. It made me feel, for the first time, like maybe I deserved some of the great things she had said about her big brother.

Don't ever tell her I said that.

"What can we do?" she yelled as the wind shrieked with renewed fury. "The basilisk is right behind us!"

"Then we won't look that way! How fast can a basilisk charge?"

"I do not know!"

"Let's hope they're slower than we are. Which way's home, again?"

Kari jogged her head to indicate the direction. I reached out, grabbed her free hand, and we started running as fast as we could. Kari's hand gripped mine so hard it hurt, but if I had learned anything at all today it was that I knew we could make it if we stuck together and kept trying. Letting go just wasn't an option. Not anymore.

Kari was *my* strange, crazy, brave, and strong sister. I wasn't leaving her behind.

Something very, very close to us that definitely wasn't human screamed over the sound of the wind. With the storm howling like a banshee now and branches falling all around, I had no way of knowing if the basilisk was gaining on us. The ground shook continuously, though whether from the coils of the basilisk close behind or from large branches slamming to earth on all sides I couldn't tell.

A branch the size of a decent tree dropped out of the murk, crashing down so close that Kari and I had to dodge to one side. My foot slipped on wet leaves as I skidded sideways and I almost fell, but Kari's grip on my hand kept me up and steadied me enough to keep going, knowing my slip had slowed us down and wondering if I was really feeling the hot breath of a basilisk very close behind. Something snagged at the back of my clothes as we went around the branch. I jerked free without looking back, Kari pulling me forward with her as she kept running, the sword in her other hand shining amid the horrible gloom.

One of the giant trees ahead of us uttered a tremendous series of bangs like a ragged volley of cannon fire as its trunk cracked. With a huge moan the whole massive tree began falling. Falling just in front of us, trying to cut us off from home. I didn't think I could run any faster, but I did, putting everything into a final burst of speed, while Kari somehow ran even faster than me and pulled me along.

A hissing filled my ears even over the wind and the crackling groan of ancient wood breaking as the tree fell like the giant it was. If you've ever stood next to a skyscraper, imagine one of those toppling sideways toward you. We crossed under the still-falling tree as I wondered how far we would have to go to clear its trunk and branches, and how close behind us the basilisk now was. Then the tree trunk hit and the earth jumped beneath us like a frightened cat. Kari and I both almost fell, but we kept our feet somehow and ran onward, blinded for a moment by showers of leaves from the fallen tree.

We ran into an open, grassy area and the wind stopped. There were only a couple of trees and we could see the stars again.

We both stumbled to a stop, gasping for breath after our run and staring around us. I couldn't hear any sounds of pursuit, so I turned very slowly. Nothing there but a wooden fence that was overdue for the repainting I had promised Dad I would get around to someday. "We made it. We're in our backyard. You got us back, Kari."

Kari started laughing very softly even though she looked like she was about to cry. "We are home. You brought me home, Liam."

Before I knew what she was doing, Kari slammed her sword into its scabbard, then with both hands free wrapped me in a hug so tight I thought my ribs were going to pop.

Okay, I sort of hugged her back. But only for a second. Because we had just escaped death and everything, you know.

"You are the bravest, strongest, and best brother ever," Kari whispered, then seemed to realize what she was doing and broke the hug, jumping back from me. "I mean...thank you, dearest brother."

"I think you had a lot to do with us getting home," I said, feeling really awkward. Man, if somebody had seen me hugging my own sister like that I would have had to spend the next ten years in hiding.

Remembering something from our run, I cautiously felt my back, finding a rip in my jeans pocket. I pulled out my wallet. There was a jagged scratch running down its length.

Kari used one finger to trace the path of the scratch. "The mark of a basilisk's fang. It seems the beast *was* rather close at the end, Liam," she noted, her voice shaking a little.

"Yeah. Thanks for holding on to me back there."

"The credit is yours, dearest brother. You were holding on to me."

"No, no, when that thing almost grabbed me, *you* were holding on to *me*."

"No, I wasn't!" Kari insisted.

"Yes, you—"

"Liam?" I saw Mom's silhouette against the light in the open kitchen door.

I looked up again at the stars. "It's late. Real late. Mom's going to be very, very upset."

Kari grinned. "She cannot be any worse than a basilisk."

"You don't know Mom when she's very, very upset." But we couldn't exactly turn around and go back to face the basilisk, so I faced the house. "Here, Mom," I called.

"Liam? Are you...are you...alone?"

"No. Of course not. Kari's here. I brought her back. I told you I would and I did."

Kari gave me a startled look. "The third promise, Liam. You have fulfilled the third promise."

Oh, yeah. Three for three. Our quest was successful and we were both home. "All right, I admit it. The Archimaede was right."

Mom stepped back to let us into the kitchen, eyeing our clothes, which bore the marks of a day involving a lot of traveling on foot through wild fields and forests, encounters with various beasts and the occasional monster or dragon, a vicious storm between worlds, and a very near miss with a basilisk. "You're pretty late getting back from that little walk."

I started to give some sarcastic answer but saw the strain still visible on Mom's face. All she had had to do was worry about us. Yeah. That's all. I had never really thought about that before, but now I could remember how I had felt when Kari had disappeared in the castle. "I'm sorry, Mom. I honestly didn't know things would be this complicated today."

"Complicated?" Mom poured herself some tea, offered some to us, but then stood there at the kitchen table like she couldn't move. She lowered her face into her hands for a moment, her voice muffled. "I can't tell you how hard it has been the last few hours."

"Mom. I'm really sorry."

She looked up and tried to smile at us. Kari had kept standing there like a soldier, and I figured I had to stand by her to keep her from feeling like a dope. Mom raised her eyebrows when she realized what we were doing. "Why haven't you two—Are you waiting for me to sit down first?"

"Of course, honored Mother," Kari replied.

Mom looked at me.

"I'm just making sure Kari's comfortable," I replied.

"Wow," Mom said. I wasn't sure what that meant. "But you two don't have to stand on ceremony at home. Sit down, please." After we had all sat down, Kari tasted her tea tentatively, then smiled. "Do you like that, Kari?"

"Yes, honored Mother."

"It's herbal tea. I thought you might like it from what I'd seen of you earlier." Mom looked away for a moment. "It wasn't easy wondering if I'd see you again. Especially when it started getting dark. Okay, you two. What have you been up to while I've been here worried sick?"

There are times to stand tall and times to pass the buck to someone else. There was no way Mom would believe me if I told the story, so I quickly pointed to Kari. "Uh, Mom, I bet Kari would do a lot better job of telling you than I would. Especially if there are any parts in elvish."

Kari didn't seem in the least put out by being put on the hot seat. "There should not be any parts in elvish," she told me.

Kari stood up, stepped back from the table, raised her open hands about even with her shoulders, palms up, and started half-singing/half-talking. "Witness all here the tale of Liam the Steadfast Brother, Keeper of Promises, He Who Fights Without a Sword," she sang, "and his sister once unknown and yet known to him, Kari, She Who was Born to Elven-kind, Bearer of the Sword of Fate, Spirit Daughter of White Lady of Eveness, She Who Was Once Apart. Listen as I tell of the perils they have overcome, frustrating the evil designs of Lady Meyer of the grim fortress of Hillcrest, crossing the terrifying walls between the worlds, fighting unwavering against the wolves of Graysinder, destroying the Demon Mirror of Lady Amelia's Keep, facing down the Elves of the Westerwood, standing firm against the spells of the Wight of the River Crossing, slaying the dragon guardian of the rock from the Moon, finding lost items of great portent, and together challenging and overcoming the grim basilisks which stood between them and their home. Listen and wonder as I sing of their exploits."

Mom just sat and stared, her mouth often hanging half open again, as Kari sang her way through what had happened. Kari had to pause at times as she improvised the next verse, but never for long. She kept her lower body pretty much in place, but used her arms, hands, and upper body to act out stuff, which made it pretty cool to watch as well as listen to.

Finally, Kari ended in grand style. "This do I sing, and this do I swear to be true on my honor and on my sword." She paused, then swept into that graceful kneel of hers, facing Mom, her head down and arms extended.

It took Mom a moment to recover. "Umm...thank you, Kari. That was...an interesting story." She looked over at me. "Am I to understand that *you* are the Steadfast Brother and Keeper of Promises?"

"Yeah." I probably sounded a little defensive, but who wouldn't?

"He is everything I sang of and more," Kari said from her kneel, raising her head to look at Mom again. "Honored Mother, if you could only have seen my brother Liam when we faced our greatest perils. You would be so proud of him. I am certain of it."

Mom smiled at both of us. "As a matter of fact, Kari, I am proud of him."

Cool. But I pointed at Kari. "She played down what she did," I insisted. "Kari did a lot more than me. She broke the mirror—"

"After you saved me from its spell," Kari interrupted, still kneeling.

"And if she hadn't gone after that dragon so hard and killed it—"

"You distracted and dazed the monster, thus saving us both."

"All right." Mom waved her hands to stop us. "Kari, please get up. We don't usually kneel in this family. Who is this White Lady of—?"

"Eveness," Kari said, standing. "She raised me, honored Mother. Shall I sing of her beauty, her grace, her flowing mane and tail, her shining horn and hooves—"

"Horn? Hooves?"

"She's a unicorn," I explained. "A real tough, mom unicorn. You'd probably like her. She talks a lot like you."

"Talks?" Mom rubbed her face for a moment, then looked at both of us. "Kari, that was really lovely, and I've never had an excuse for getting home late sung and performed for me. It's also unusual to hear a brother and a sister competing to say nice things about each other. But, let me make one thing absolutely clear." She raised one hand, the forefinger extended toward us. "I would not believe one single word of this story—"

"Mom!"

"Honored Mother!"

"—if Kari wasn't here telling it." Mom shook her head as she looked at Kari. "Compared to you being here, compared to the daughter I never had showing up in my life, things like talking unicorns and dragons don't seem all that remarkable."

"Your pardon, honored Mother, but why are talking unicorns hard for you to accept?"

Mom twisted her mouth as she thought. That's when I finally realized where Kari got that expression from. "I've never met one, Kari," she said.

"That won't be the case much longer," I said, thinking of what White Lady had told Kari about coming to visit.

"Uh huh. Sure." Mom shook her head once more. "What I meant, Kari, is that compared to you being here, nothing else seems all that impossible. If you can walk into this family from out of nowhere—"

"Elsewhere," Kari and I both said at the same time.

"Jinx," I added, "you owe me a soda."

"I owe you a what?" Kari asked. "Am I under a geas?"

"No," I assured her. "I'll let it pass this time."

"My dearest brother has been telling me about this world," Kari explained to Mom.

"That's nice." Mom looked like she was about to laugh. "That's very nice of you, uh, dearest brother Liam. So, you came from Elsewhere, Kari. The point is, I can't think of any possible simpler explanation for you, Kari, and as for you, Liam, if you were going to make up a story to explain where you were, I think you'd have picked something a little less bizarre."

"It really is the truth, Mom," I said.

"Truly, honored Mother," Kari added.

Mom sighed. "All right, call me crazy, but I believe your story." Then she raised a warning finger once more, her face stern. "But let me make sure of one thing. Neither of you is planning to make a habit of wandering around other worlds fighting dragons and then getting back home late, right?"

Kari and I both nodded. "Only if the fate of the universe is hanging in the balance again," I said.

"Sure," Mom said. "Even then, you'd better count on getting permission. Well, I guess I can overlook it this once. Next time you tell me you're just going for a walk, though, I'm going to demand a little more information before you leave this house."

I grinned. "You're the greatest, Mom."

Mom snorted and looked skeptical. "Are you going to start calling me 'honored Mother', too?"

"Do I have to?"

"No. Neither do you, Kari. As much as I like hearing you say it, just having you call me Mother is enough to take my breath away. We've got a spare bedroom," Mom continued. "It'll be yours now."

And then Mom looked at me like she expected some comment.

"What?" I asked.

"You don't have any objection to Kari getting the spare bedroom?"

"Why would I object to that?"

Mom looked at me for a moment longer, then smiled again. "No reason. No reason at all. I can't wait for your Father to get home tonight."

"Tonight?" I asked. "I thought he wasn't coming home until the weekend."

"He called to say he was getting home early. I left you a message about it on your phone."

"My phone?" I spread my hands apologetically. "I lost it, Mom."

"Oh. Yeah." Mom rested her chin on one hand as she looked at me. "The enchanted phone that saved you and Kari from those elves. I guess we'll have to get you a new one. But that's a lot of money, Liam. We'll need to try to make a claim on the replacement policy. I donh't think it covers encounters with elves, so we'll have to say something else, like a bear broke it when you were hiking."

"Um...Mom, we shouldn't lie about it. I can wait a few months until we can afford a replacement. It's just a phone. I can live without it."

Mom stared at me, like I had said something completely bizarre, then grinned. "You're right, Liam. We shouldn't lie about it, and we can live without it." Mom switched her gaze to Kari. "He's only spent one day with you."

I wasn't sure just what that meant, and Kari didn't know what to make of it, either. "It was a very long day, honored Mother," she said.

Silence fell for a moment, and I realized that it seemed like a million years had gone by since this morning, when we had been in this same kitchen and I had been trying to figure out how to ditch this strange girl as fast as possible because she didn't belong in my life. Maybe my life was a little bigger and contained a lot more than I had realized. Maybe by giving up a few things, I had gained a lot of other things.

I was still thinking about that when I heard a car pulling into the driveway.

"There's your father," Mom said.

Kari gasped and put her hand to her heart. "Father."

Mom smiled at her again. "I wasn't sure what to tell him when he got here. But now I've got you two."

I took a deep breath. "How are you going to tell him?"

Mom got a really wicked expression on her face. "The same way I found out. Come on. Your father's got a surprise coming." She took Kari's hand and led her toward the front door.

I followed quickly. No way I wanted to miss this.

We stood in the entry, waiting. The front door's lock turned, the door opened, and Dad stepped in. He shut the door and looked at each of us in turn. "Hi, darling. Hi, Liam. Hi, Kari." Dad turned enough to toss his briefcase on the hall table. "Liam and Kari didn't have to stay up for me, even though it's nice to see you all—"

His voice cut off and Dad froze. Like, motionless.

His head turned really slowly until he was looking at Kari again where she stood next to Mom. "*Our daughter?*"

Mom nodded, smiling cheerfully. "Yes. I still don't entirely understand how, but she is your daughter and mine. She's fourteen, by the way."

Dad's eyes went back to Kari and stayed there a while before he said anything else. "Kari. You...have a sword."

Kari smiled tentatively. "Yes, honored Father."

"What have you been doing all this time? Why do you have a sword? Where have you been?"

I held up both hands. "It's a long story, Dad."

"Yes," Mom agreed. "Well worth listening to and seeing, by the way, but I expect that Kari is a little too tired to go through it again tonight. What counts right now is the ending, which is here. It has ended, hasn't it, Kari? Is anything else supposed to happen?"

Kari bit her lip, She stepped back and went into her graceful kneel, head bowed and hands clasped before her, facing both Mom and Dad. "That is up to you, honored Mother and Father."

"What do you mean?"

Kari kept her head lowered as she spoke. "I am here...but I will remain within these walls only if you wish me to stay."

Mom looked as if she couldn't decide whether to laugh or cry. "If we wish you to stay? Kari, sweetheart, of course we want you here, always."

"Told you so," I reminded Kari.

Mom went down on her knees and hugged Kari. "I've spent so many years wondering where you were." Mom looked surprised. "I did! I didn't know you were anywhere, but I wondered where you were. I never realized that until now."

"It is very complicated," Kari admitted, raising her head and gazing at Mom. "The Archimaede told me once that even the walls between worlds could not completely block a mother's sight. I did not know what that meant."

"I think I do. Do you understand it now?"

"Yes." Kari the dragon slayer looked as if she was going to cry. "Honored Father?"

Dad grinned. "As if there's any question. Welcome home, Kari."

Then Dad gave me a stern look.

"What?" I asked.

Dad indicated Kari. "You've got a sister, Liam. That's a big change. You're no longer the only child. We'll have to think about her, too, from now on."

"Yeah. Sure."

"There'll be more expenses. We'll have to put off getting a new TV."

"Yeah. So?"

Dad looked at Mom, puzzled. "Have you already talked about this?"

"I didn't have to," Mom said. "I think you have Kari and Liam to thank for his change in attitude."

"You don't have any problem with her coming into our home?" Dad asked me, sounding like he didn't believe what he was saying.

"Problem? What kind of brother do you think I am? Kari is my sister. She's got my back. And I've got her back. End of story."

And that was that.

Chapter Nine

HOME AGAIN, HOME AGAIN

 SO, NOW I'VE GOT A SISTER. IT TURNED OUT I'D ALWAYS SORT of had a sister, which I admit is unusual for an only child, but now I really have one.

The morning after fighting for my life and the existence of two universes I had to get up for school just as usual. Being sore and bruised and tired from fighting dragons and junk wasn't an excuse for missing school. Kari offered to strap on her sword and escort me just in case the evil Lady Meyer tried to suspend me over the pits in her dungeon, but I told her that I'd be okay.

At school, James wouldn't even talk to me. It wasn't too hard to figure out why. What with all that quest stuff and narrowly escaping death in the coils of a basilisk I never had called him to go over that book report. When we went to English class I walked right up to Mr. Weedle and explained that I had promised to help James with his report but hadn't done it, and if Mr. Weedle wanted to fail me that was only fair, but would he please give James a few more days to do his report, which I really would help him with this time. Weedle looked at me for several very long seconds, then told me that James and I both had three more days to get the report in, even though we would both get minus ten points on our grades for it being late. Which was really decent of Weedle, I thought.

And James seemed to think I had done something special, even though I told him that it was really the only right thing to do. It wasn't easy going up to Weedle like that, but when there's something you know you have to do, you ought to face up to it and get it done. Especially when someone else is counting on you. That's what I always say.

We got those reports done, too, just like I said we would, even though I kept having this urge to stay out of James's reach. "Do you think I'm going to hit you or something?" he demanded.

No, I think you might be a wight trying to lure me into your cold hole. Nah, probably shouldn't say that.

That spare bedroom I had so many plans for is Kari's now, all decked out with tapestries and her enchanted Sword of Fate and other girl stuff like that. She's made a new minstrel's harp (they sell kits for that, believe it or not). The upstairs bathroom is a lot more crowded, too, because Kari did put a lot of stuff in there, but I can live with that.

Dad is sometimes a bit overwhelmed by Kari, but that's just the effect she has on most people. I found out what he does at work. Don't tell anyone, but it's actually kind of interesting. And it turns out he used to play fantasy game stuff, too, when he was a kid. How weird is that?

Mom's so happy that I'd be jealous if it weren't for the fact that Kari had saved me from being dragon kibble. Besides, I've been thinking about Kari, growing up not even knowing where Mom was. Thinking about all the things I would have missed if it had been me. Along with missing a lot of rules and lectures, of course, though from what Kari says White Lady had plenty of rules of her own.

The strange thing is that Mom is giving me a lot more slack now. She says it's not about me being nicer to her (and I'm trying, after realizing what it would have been like without Mom around) but because I've been showing she can trust me. Which doesn't make much sense, since I haven't really changed, have I?

A lot of birds hang around the house, which bothered Mom and Dad at first, because they thought it was a little weird to have a daughter who talked to birds. But I told them that Kari had recruited the birds as scouts and was using them as a sort of neighborhood watch. Once Mom and Dad heard that they decided Kari's bird friends were all right after all.

James hasn't had any problem with Kari. As a matter of fact, he seems to like her. A lot. I need to keep an eye on him.

Oh, and I managed to convince Kari that Principal Meyer isn't an evil dungeon master. When I eventually brought her to school Kari and Meyer circled each other like a pair of lionesses who were trying to decide if they should have a fight to the death or not, but once they got used to each other Kari decided Meyer wasn't that bad and once Kari started winning sports awards Meyer decided Kari was all right too. She plays on the school lacrosse team, runs track like nobody's business, and has started a club to teach kids at the school how to use swords. Including Tina. "Because a girl never knows when she might need a sword, Liam," Kari told me.

And now Tina talks to me. Tina really likes Kari, and seems to think Kari's brother is worth knowing, too, which is seriously cool. "I'm sorry I froze you out, Liam, but before I met Kari I thought you were kind of a jerk."

I don't know where she could have gotten that idea, but now that she knows me things are cool. Who am I to argue with that?

So now we're just a typical family, and even though Kari misses her old home, she still gets to visit with old friends.

"Liam, tell your sister that unicorn is in the backyard again!"

Kari bolted past me down the stairs while Mom got a punch bowl full of ice water and a plate of fruit salad for the unicorn. White Lady also likes oatmeal cookies, it turns out. We all sat out back and talked about things, just me, my sister, my Mom and the unicorn, while birds flew down to perch on Kari.

I know. Kari's still a bit weird. But isn't every little sister at least a little weird?

ABOUT THE AUTHOR

JACK CAMPBELL (JOHN G. HEMRY) IS THE AUTHOR OF THE New York Times best-selling *Lost Fleet* series, the *Lost Stars* series, and the "steampunk with dragons" *Pillars of Reality* Series. His most recent books are *The Lost Stars: Shattered Spear, The Lost Fleet: Beyond the Frontier - Leviathan,* and the *Pillars of Reality* novels *The Servants of the Storm* and *The Wrath of the Great Guilds*. In May, *Vanguard* will be published, the first in a new trilogy set centuries before the events in *The Lost Fleet* series. John's novels have been published in eleven languages. This year, Titan will begin bringing out a *Lost Fleet* comic series. His short fiction includes works covering time travel, alternate history, space opera, military SF, fantasy, and humor.

John has also written articles on declassified Cold War plans for US military bases on the Moon, and *Liberating the Future: Women in the Early Legion (of Superheroes) in Sequart's Teenagers From the Future*. At somewhat erratic intervals he presents his talk on *Everything I Needed To Know About Quantum Physics I Learned From The Three Stooges*, showing how Stooge skits illustrate principles of quantum physics.

John is a retired US Navy officer, who served in a wide variety of jobs including surface warfare (the ship drivers of the Navy), amphibious warfare, anti-terrorism, intelligence, and some other things that he's not supposed to talk about. Being a sailor, he has been known to tell stories about Events Which He Says Really Happened (but which cannot be verified by any independent sources). This experience has served him well in writing fiction.

He lives in Maryland with his indomitable wife "S" and three great kids (all three on the autism spectrum).

Post-Apocalyptic, Coming-of-Age Backers

Alexander "Guddha" Gudenau
Amelia F. Dudley
Amelia Smith
Amy zortman
Anders M. Ytterdahl
Andreas Gustafsson
Andres Salazar
Andrew Topperwien
Ann Wiewall
Anonymous
Anonymous
Aramanth Dawe
B."Commodore Stargazer" Whitcraft
Becky B
Bill Markley
Brenda Cooper
Brendan Lonehawk
Brian Lintz
Calvin Coolidge
Carina Bissett
Carmen Maria Marin
Carol A. Andrescavage
Cathy Schwartz
Chad Bowden
Cheri Kannarr
Christopher J. Burke
Christopher S. Sanders
Colleen R. Cahill
Craig Girten
Crazy Lady Used Books & Emporium
Cullen Gilchrist
Curtis and Maryrita Steinhour
Cynthia J. Radthorne
Cynthia Porter
Daniel Lin
Dave Lewis
David Amerson
David Cooper
David Edelstein
David Holden
David Lee Summers
David Mortman
David Perlmutter
David Perkins
David Weinman
Deena Cates
Dina S. Willner
Dirk
D-Rock
Duncan Campbell

Elizabeth Crefin
Elizabeth Inglee-Richards
Erin Penn
Gary Clark
Gavran
Gisele Peterson
Isaac 'Will It Work' Dansicker
Jakub Narębski
James Rowland
Janet Oblinger
Janito Vaqueiro Ferreira Filho
Janka Hobbs
Jason Genser
Jen
Jennifer Brozek
Jennifer Ihrke
Jeremy Brett
Jeremy Reppy
Jeremy Tolbert
Jesse kilgore
Jessica Reid
Joe Anders
John Green
John Idlor
Joshua Palmatier
Joy Adiletta
Joyce Ann Garcia from
McAllen Texas
Judy Waidlich
Julianna Hinckley
K.c. Ball
Karen Dubois
Karen Shaw
Kat Wing
Kate Baker
Katherine Malloy
Kay Pease
Kerry aka Trouble
Kori Flint
Laurie Hicks
Lawrence M. Schoen

Lennhoff Family
Lisa Kruse
Mae McKinnon
Margaret McGraw
Margaret Coin
Margaret M. St. John
Mark Carter
Mark F Goldfield
Mark Hirschman
Mark Knapp
Mark Lukens
Mary
Mary Alice Wuerz
Mat Masding-Grouse
Matt P
Michael Jan Friedman
Mike Moscoe
Mike Thurlow
Molly Kate McGinn
Nicole van Niekerk
Paul Ryan
Paul van Oven
Peter Donald
Ralph M. Seibel
Raymond Finch
Rene Sears
Revek
Rhel
Rich Walker
RKBookman
Robby Thrasher
Robert E. Stein
Robert Early
Robert T. Bryson
Ryan Riley
Scott Schaper
Shervyn
Sheryl R. Hayes
Stash LaBrake
Stephanie Bissette-Roark
Stephen Ballentine

Stephen Cheng
Steven Mentzel
Susan Carlson
Susan R Grossman
Svend Andersen
SwordFire
thatraja
The Filipovichs
The Geek Girl Project
THE Kevin
The Kline Family

Thomas Bull
Tina M Noe-Good
Tom B.
Tom Crepeau
Tom Hunt
Trip Space-Parasite
Vickie DiSanto
Vincent L. Cleaver
Whitney Parker
William G Boegly
William Seney

CPSIA information can be obtained
at www.ICGtesting.com
Printed in the USA
LVOW11s0043120517

534238LV00001B/120/P

9 781942 990406